Blue Honor

A female Russian spy holds the key to finding Vander's brother. Can he trust her?

Navy SEAL Vander Knight usually relies on fear and intimidation to extract intel from an enemy, but his standard tactics won't work on the red-headed spitfire he's tasked with questioning.

He'll have to resort to building rapport with his sexy prisoner to coax her into revealing her secrets.

Breaking Misha without falling for her may be the toughest battle he'll ever face, but with his brother's life on the line, failure is not an option.

Misha refuses to yield to the demands of the gorgeous commando who has taken her captive.

Even if he bribes her with a sweet stray puppy, she won't tell him anything about her double life as a Russian agent.

She'll simply retaliate with a seduction that will bring him to his knees.

Vander may be a worthy opponent, but he's not the only one who can fight dirty.

If a handsome, mysterious man asked you how you'd like your drink, would you choose neat, on the rocks, or shaken and stirred with a twist of danger? I know which one I'd pick. — Bex Dane

Chapter 1 The Mistress

Cartagena, Colombia

Misha/Skyler

My soul shriveled as he pumped his tiny dick.

His grunt into my neck told me it was over.

At least it never lasted long.

He pulled out without kissing me. "I have to leave right away."

And he usually left quickly after.

Did that make it any better? No. Nothing could take this stain off me. I'd wear it like a scar for the rest of my life.

Ruben Duran, a vile Colombian drug lord, pulled on his ugly tighty-whities and a pair of black pants that barely closed around his protruding belly.

I wiped off with the sheet and quickly dressed.

"Going anywhere special?" I asked him as I slipped on my heels.

His moustache twisted with his smirk. "I shouldn't tell you this, but we've captured an American."

"Oh." What a wretched, dreadful man. "It sounds dangerous."

He nodded as he buttoned up his shirt over the dingy tank top he never removed and the tasteless gold chains around his neck. "They'll pay to get him back."

Ransom for an American? Ruben was taking his crime ring to a whole new level. "Aren't you already the wealthiest man in Colombia?"

He straightened his pinky ring with a snake imprinted on it. "The more money, the better off my children will be."

That's right. Ruben Duran did everything "for his children." Or so he said. The truth was he ran off pure greed and hunger for power in a useless attempt to soothe his insecurities.

He kissed my lips and bile rose in my throat. "I love you, my sweet Skyler."

I hated the name Skyler, particularly from his mouth. I was not Skyler. I was Misha. Whoever she was.

"Love you too, Ruben." I was dead inside. Sometimes I wished I would be exposed, so I could have an excuse to die. I'd come close to doing it myself, but it was the one murder I could not carry out.

I lived a miserable existence, but some intrinsic part of my psyche couldn't relinquish the will to live.

Ruben pointed to a young man standing outside my window. "I'm putting four guards on your villa."

"Really? Why?"

"I feel like I'm being followed."

Ah, the ubiquitous paranoia that came with a life of crime.

"When will I see you again?" I twirled my finger over the coarse gray hair above his ear hoping he'd say months. A year would be nice.

"Two weeks."

Darn.

"Can't wait." We embraced, his belly poking my abdomen since I was taller than him with my heels on. I leaned down so he could kiss me with his wrinkled lips.

He turned and left without saying goodbye.

I locked the door behind him and fought the turmoil in my heart as I sat on the end of the bed. How much longer could I keep up this ruse? Every week I waited for Sergei's order to kill Ruben, but it never came. Only instructions to keep working my way closer to him. He'd said he loved me. I was his favorite mistress. How much closer did I need to be?

I'd give anything to fly away from here and start a new life where Russia and the Agency didn't exist. I'd be a normal girl with everyday problems. Going on dates in the city, ordering a latte in a coffee shop, maybe working in an office somewhere having a torrid affair with the boss. Not this facade of a woman who wasn't even sure who she was without a disguise.

A scratch outside my window caught my attention. I peeked out in time to see Ruben's guard collapse with a thud, his head bouncing off the pavement, his eyes wide and unfocused, a line of blood seeping from his slashed neck. My peripheral vision picked up the movement of a shadow, but I didn't see it so much as I felt it.

Someone was out there.

An attack.

An ambush.

Who? It could be one of Ruben's many enemies or perhaps it was the Americans looking to retaliate for the kidnapping. Americans did not mess around and Ruben was playing with fire.

I grabbed my rifle and took up a defensive position next to the bed. I had a full magazine loaded and a round chambered in ten seconds. No one would get through that door without a bullet in his head.

Chapter 2 Hellcat

Vander/Viper

"He added four guards." I spoke to my team through the mic in my ear as Ruben Duran left his mistress's villa.

"So we take 'em out," Magnum, my second-in-command, replied.

"Shit." We'd planned to capture her without being noticed. Gunshots in the early morning hours would wake the neighborhood and draw too much attention.

As expected, Plan A was dust.

"Got your Kabars?" I pulled my seven-inch military knife from its sheath in my side pocket. Magnum prepared his, and I heard several affirmatives through my earpiece.

"I'll take the tango on the west side," I announced. The man in front of her window would be dead in minutes.

"East is mine," Magnum replied.

"We'll take the two on the south end." Axel and London were positioned around the back of the villa.

Adrenaline flooded through my body, my heartrate picked up, and I struggled to keep my breathing under control.

Finally, it was go-time after weeks of surveillance and waiting.

We'd done this a thousand times. No need to be nervous. But this op was different. It was personal.

My missing brother's life was on the line.

Every action had to be calculated and precise. No room for screw ups.

"Ready. Move."

We approached under the cover of the moonless night. Silent footsteps on pavement. My target was young and inattentive. An easy kill.

I stepped up behind him, pulled him off balance with an arm around his neck, and then sliced it. I released him and slid into the shadows. He fell within a few seconds, no idea what hit him.

Magnum's victim's eyes widened before he faced the same fate.

The distinct sound of two other throats being sliced followed in my earpiece.

Four down.

Magnum and I stepped over the bodies and took position on opposite sides of the wooden door that was the last barrier between my team and our target.

Gunfire popped from inside the villa and shrapnel pierced the wood of the door.

We hit the ground. "We're taking fire," I called on the comms. "She was supposed to be in there alone. What the hell?"

"She's alone. She's fucking firing at us," Magnum said.

"Holy shit."

We couldn't return fire because we needed to take this target alive.

The shooting paused.

"We go non-lethal. Make sure she doesn't bleed out." I took the risk of rising to take a quick look through the window. The glass above my head shattered and I dropped back down. "No shot. No line of sight."

"Stand by," Axel called through the comms. A few seconds later, the lights in the villa clicked off. "Power's cut."

"Excellent." This left her alone in the dark.

I snapped down my night vision goggles. My field of vision turned green. I could see her, but she couldn't see me. "I'm going for it. Cover me."

Magnum stood with his back against the wall and nodded. It was an insane plan, but the only move we had.

"I'll provide a distraction from the rear," Axel said.

"On my count." I adjusted my rifle over my back. "Three, two, one!"

Magnum kicked the door near the lock and it swung open. She fired wildly as I rounded the entry corner on my belly, keeping low and tight to the wall.

The back of the house rocked with an explosion.

I was almost to her.

My knee struck something and a lamp crashed to the floor.

Her torso swayed in my direction.

Shots blew past my head as I scrambled to get to her before she hit me.

She paused to listen and I quieted my breathing, but the scrape of my pants on the carpet gave me away.

She fired, and ow, fuck, hit my arm. "Son of a bitch, motherfucker."

I climbed to one knee and sprung on her.

Fire streaked through my arm as we collided and slammed into the wall.

I dislodged her rifle and tossed it, pulling some of her hair with it.

We grappled in a tight corner beside the bed.

With a feral growl, sharp claws swiped a long track down my neck. I grabbed her wrist and forced it over her head.

Taking advantage of my injury, she bent her shoulder and twisted out of my grasp.

What a little pain in my ass this one was.

In an ungraceful move, I knocked her to her stomach by smashing my torso to her back.

She grunted and screamed as she kicked her heels into my spine and rammed her elbow into my injured arm.

What a damn hellcat. Fighting to avoid capture despite being pinned and covered by a team of armed operators.

I'd totally underestimated this woman. A major screw up we couldn't afford.

Magnum kneeled on her ankles. "Need help there, Stud?"

"Shut up and get her out of here." I pushed off her and moved aside.

Magnum flipped her to her back and held her wrists over her head. She dug her nails into his hands and hissed.

"Down, gatita." Magnum called her the Spanish word for kitten.

She spit in his face.

The woman was no kitten. She was a rabid T-Rex who'd just tried to kill me.

I motioned for Jade, our only female operator on this mission, to assist Magnum. She struggled to zip-cuff the woman's wrists and ankles.

When Jade lifted her by her armpits, she went limp, her ass hanging low and knees bent. She braced all her weight on the tips of the tall stiletto heels she'd managed to keep on during our tussle.

Magnum tucked a shoulder into her chest and lifted her in a fireman's carry. He smiled as he jogged out with her writhing body around his shoulders, red heels kicking to break free, hair flying wild.

Not fucking funny.

Not at all.

This hellcat was our key to finding my brother.

And it was my job to break her.

***

We took her to the safe house outside Cartagena. Magnum carried the woman to the room we used for detainees, and Jade stayed with her. It had the basics. A bed, bathroom, and bars over the windows.

London, our team medic, injected a local anesthetic and patched up the flesh wound beneath my left bicep. "You're lucky she's a bad shot."

"I don't think she is." For the entire thirty-minute ride to the safe house, the woman seethed as she sat with Jade on a bench across from me. "If the lights were on or she had NVG, we'd all be dead."

"She was quite impressive," he said, his British accent making the compliment seem polite.

In any other situation, I'd share some admiration of her skills with him. However, she'd tried to kill me, and it was sheer chance that bullet didn't penetrate my face or neck instead of grazing my bicep. A SEAL never forgot or forgave. No one had ever shot at me and survived for long.

"She's lucky to be alive after that bullshit. Many times I held back from shooting her myself."

London finished working and started applying ointment and a bandage to my wound. "But she's our key to Duran. Hopefully he's chatty after he blows his load."

"We underestimated her. She's not just some woman who has Duran by the balls. She's trained. Why did he put four guards on her?"

"I liked her too." Magnum walked into the kitchen and grabbed a bottle of water.

"Oh really? She won you over by spitting in your face and digging her nails into you?"

"Yeah." He laughed and stuck his tongue out.

Magnum earned his nickname by going through condoms faster than the store on base could supply them. We'd all noticed her assets. "Keep your dick out of my hostage."

"Will do," he threw out as he left the kitchen.

"Even if we knew why Duran was guarding her, it's irrelevant." London returned to the conversation as he wiped hydrogen peroxide over the bloody scrapes on my neck. "All that matters is what she knows about Steel."

Right. The woman was distracting me, but I couldn't get over how she was so different from what I'd expected.

"Steel is the only reason she's alive right now." I glared at the door to the room where Jade was working with her. She would play the good cop by offering her food and clothes. Then I'd come in and remind her who she was dealing with.

Normally I'd go easy on a woman, but when this one tried to kill me, she became just like any other enemy. She'd get no mercy from me.

"Don't stress that wound or get it dirty," London warned as he tossed supplies in the trash and packed up his kit.

"Right."

"I'm serious. If it gets infected..."

"I'll be fine by tomorrow."

He held his tongue on what he wanted to say. I knew how to take care of a wound, and I knew exactly what to do with the hellcat in the other room.

Chapter 3 Death Wish

Skyler/Misha

"My name is Jade. I'm going to take these off of you so you can use the restroom, eat, and sleep." The woman spoke in Spanish as she removed the zip-cuffs from my hands and ankles.

I massaged the sore spots to rub out the pain.

"Try anything and they go back on."

They were using a familiar tactic. She'd be nice to me and offer me privileges to make me think she was on my side, and then one of her teammates would swoop in and snatch it all away. Weaken me. Place me at their mercy.

Their tricks wouldn't work. I had a lifetime of training, and too much was at risk if the Agency found out I'd failed to withstand an interrogation.

This was a test, and I had to perform as expected of an SVG agent. I couldn't let anyone discover the truth about me or my job. If I revealed anything, I'd pay with my life.

The door opened, and the soldier who'd led the attack on my villa entered the room. He was at least six-foot-seven and two hundred eighty pounds. He scowled at me, but I didn't falter. Big guys were usually all bluster and no bite.

He shared an unspoken word with Jade and moved his eyes to me as she left the room.

"Cuál es tu nombre?" He asked me my name in Spanish.

"Eat shit and die," I replied in English and crossed my arms over my chest.

His brow wrinkled. "You speak English?"

13

I leaned back in my chair and spread my legs. "You catch on quick there, G.I. Joe. You must be the smart one of the group."

The way his astonished eyes focused between my legs struck me as comical. Like a malfunctioning robot attempting to handle an anomaly. Error. Error. Does not compute.

He set his jaw, and his brow scrunched into a series of wrinkled lines. "What's your name?" he asked in English as if the robot had decided repeating the question was the best solution.

I swiped the tangled hair out of my face and stared at him with an impassive expression.

He was good-looking for a jarhead, if that's what he was. The fatigues he wore earlier were unmarked, and now he wore gray cargo pants and a tight black tee. He had thick dark hair, deep-set light brown eyes, a scruffy jaw, a slightly bent nose, and a jagged scar on his face.

Darn. A handsome man was harder to seduce, and this man was gorgeous. He'd be overly familiar with women flirting and attempting to entice him to do what they wanted. My ace in the hole would likely be useless against him. If seduction was off the table, I had to find another way to crack this iceberg.

Machismo men like him always lacked confidence and I knew how to capitalize on it. Nothing shook an insecure man more than a brave woman. I had to remain strong. If I caused him to question himself and he lowered his guard, I could procure his weapon and hold him at gunpoint while I broke through a window.

His frosty gaze lingered on my shoes then traveled up my body to my breasts. Maybe he was affected by me physically, and seduction was not off the table after all.

"Are you American?"

When I didn't answer, he leaned forward and took a menacing step toward me in an attempt to intimidate me.

He failed. "I have nothing to say to you."

"What's your relationship with Ruben Duran? Why did he have four men guarding you?"

I stared at him unimpressed and stone-faced. He'd have to work a lot harder to get anything out of me.

"One of your guards is still alive. We captured him. Tell me your name and he lives. Simple exchange."

Nope. Not falling for it. I challenged him with arched eyebrows. "You're bluffing, and you're not good at it either. I watched him die. You could drive spikes into my palms and nail me to this chair, and I wouldn't tell you anything. You won't though because you're American. I can tell by your cocky assumption you're in charge of everyone. You wouldn't cross the line to torture me. You won't risk it."

As I talked, his face contorted into a scowl of such ferocity, I could almost see his wires crossing until smoke came out of his ears.

"First of all, no one knows you're here, so if I torture you and dispose of the body, there would be no proof a crime was committed." He stepped closer until his weapon swayed within a foot of my grasp. This was working. He was losing his composure. "Second, I'm here with special authority that is none of your business, but if I choose to torture you to get what I need, I have carte blanche."

"You wouldn't do it. You're not man enough to hurt a woman." There. That should hit him right in the balls. If he wasn't fuming before, he would be now.

He paused and stood up straight. The robot was processing again. Loading, loading, loading. "Torturing a woman doesn't make you manly. It makes you a coward."

I waved my hand in front of me like I was gesturing, but I was really attempting to get closer to his pistol. "There you have it. If you aren't a coward, you won't hurt me." My gaze dropped to his gun. So close. One more inch.

His eyes caught me looking, and he drew the gun from his hip before I could react.

Grabbing my upper arm, he forced me off the chair and pressed my face into the bed with his knee in the small of my back. He held the gun to my temple and overextended my arm until I squealed from the pain.

"You got a death wish? Huh?"

I had to stop fighting his hold. It hurt too much, so I relaxed my muscles and let him twist my arm.

"Your life and your body are in my hands. If I decide to remove your teeth with pliers, I'll do it without hesitation. Many men have left this room crying like babies drowning in their own blood. Don't think for a second I won't hurt you because you're a woman. You shot me tonight and I'm eager to return the favor, so for the sake of your teeth, I'd advise you to keep a lid on the bullshit and choose words I'd like to hear. Understood?"

"Ugh." He could snap my shoulder right out of the socket with a tiny bit of pressure.

"Understood?" He pulled my arm back, and fire burned through it like a live wire.

"Yes."

He released me, and I groaned through the pain as I retracted my arm. I was wrong about him. Insecurity wasn't his weakness. He didn't have any human faults. He was a detached, cruel automaton.

I fully believed he would hurt me like he'd promised. I'd never be able to break through. I saw no way out of this predicament that didn't involve extreme pain and suffering for me.

"Get some sleep, Eat Shit and Die. Might be your last chance for a while. Don't try to escape. The entire unit is wired and guarded by men who have orders to kill you."

Would that be so bad? Death would be the easy way out now. I sat up and braced my weight on my palms. "Then why didn't you shoot me tonight?"

"Is that what you'd like?" He smirked like he'd be happy to do the deed.

"Yes. Do it. Kill me now and end all this. I dare you."

His lips drew back into a fake smile that made his eyes look crazy. "You answer some questions correctly then I'll grant your request. You talk, I kill you. Win-win." He left the room and slammed the door.

I collapsed down onto the bed. What did it matter who killed me? This man or one of the Agency's men? Death was the same regardless of the source of the bullet.

Now I was hoping he wasn't bluffing. Maybe I'd tell him everything and wait to see who kept their word. Sergei or the robot. Many ways to die. I just needed one of them to do it. I'd waited too long to finally escape this failed experiment that was called my life.

Chapter 4 Over and Out

Vander/Viper

When did I become this man?

A man that would hurt a woman, threaten her, scare her.

The years of living in combat zones where the laws of human decency didn't apply had blackened my soul.

I slit a man's throat tonight without hesitation or after thought. I'd been doing the same all over the world for years.

Men had died under my command, and yet I continued undeterred. Somehow brushing off responsibility under the guise of duty. My brother was in jeopardy now because of my callousness and selfishness.

I was faithful only to my country and my brothers in arms.

Anyone else was collateral damage.

Or was being a murderer my true nature? Maybe I hadn't become this man, I'd always been him. I killed my father before I even thought of joining the Navy. No remorse. No conscience.

Damn. This woman had me questioning myself. Not good. I had to brush her off and carry on, but I couldn't stop thinking of how she'd started out bravely defiant then crumbled and submitted too easily. Not that I gave her much choice, but the fight left her too fast.

She'd begged me to kill her, and I'd promised to do it without questioning it.

Had I become so out of touch with empathy that a desperate woman's pleas didn't affect me?

Before I could continue with my self-pity party, Jade walked back into the common room from the kitchen. "I'll guard her while you sleep."

Watching her enter the detainee's room shook me out of my wallowing. My team needed me to be strong. They were looking to me to guide us through this as I'd done through many other screwed up situations over the years.

I grabbed a blanket from my kit and picked a couch. As my head hit the cushion, a call came through from my contact at the Joint Special Operations Command, which was the unit officially in charge of this mission.

JSOC had given it the codename Operation Strong as Steel in honor of my brother's nickname and had multiple SEAL and Delta Force teams on the ground searching for him. So far, all efforts had turned up nothing but false alarms. That's why the woman was critical.

"Tell me you have good news," I said to Grady Morris after we'd exchanged the security passwords.

"Nothing. You?"

Why was he calling me if he had no new intel? "We have the female target in custody."

"Good."

"Four of Duran's guards engaged." In other words, dead. Under my command. My orders. It wasn't easy or okay, but it was required to save my brother. For now, I had to stuff the guilt down and focus on the goal. Finding Steel.

"So what's the purpose of this call?" I asked Grady, impatient with his silence.

He hesitated.

"Look, I have three hours to catch some shuteye before sunrise, so you wanna go ahead and say what you need to so I can get to it?"

"Fine. The CIA wants to send in a female interrogation specialist." He sounded reticent and I knew why. This news would inflame me. I hated anyone overriding my authority.

I kept my voice measured, giving him a chance to explain himself. "We have a female operative here, and I *am* an interrogation specialist." Maybe I'd misunderstood his intentions. I'd jumped down the throat of too many superiors before and had learned not to overreact until I had all the facts.

"The talk was the last three kidnappings yielded no reliable intel." His sarcastic tone said it all. He knew this was bullshit.

"The last three gave us intel that led us to her." It required threatening them with pliers, but all of Duran's men had caved and told me the mistress was controlling him. They insisted she had power over him, and she would have insight into his plans and operations.

Despite what I'd told the woman, I'd never crossed the line into physical torture. I'd made many detainees shit their pants in fear of being tortured, but physically, I left them relatively unharmed.

"I hear you and I have no doubts about your aptitude," he said.

"Then what's really going on here?" Grady needed to give it to me straight. I didn't have time for backhanded lies right now. He'd known me for years, and we'd worked dozens of ops together. If he wasn't honest with me right now, I'd have to rethink Knight Security's relationship with JSOC.

"If she learns too much, she has to be eliminated. I believe this bogus request is a set up to send in an agent to take her out if she jeopardizes our position."

I let that sink in. They wanted to send in a CIA officer like a babysitter to make sure I didn't expose their covert operations in Colombia.

"That's not how any of this works. Black ops are black for a reason. I call the shots, and I take the heat. They keep their hands clean and fake ignorance if things go south. They don't send in assassins to kill my informants." Just thinking of the implications made my blood boil. I didn't even know this woman's name, but there was no way in hell some alphabet soup agency was going to step in and kill her. I gritted my teeth and tried to hold back the anger bubbling beneath my skin. "I got this. No one knows the stakes better than me. I'll get the intel we need from her, my team will find Steel and bring him home. She will not become a liability, and they're seriously fucked for considering it. If anyone shows up here, KS walks out on JSOC and they'll be stuck with no contractor to fill their voids." I didn't like to threaten the people paying the bills, but I needed to get my point across and state the obvious. They needed me, and they shouldn't piss me off.

"Right. I'll get them to back down. They crossed a line."

"They damn well did. A line no one has crossed in the ten years I've been running these ops. Not one time has the CIA or anyone else had to send in an agent to clean up my mess. I'm the best at what I do. No one is screwing this up for me or my team, especially not this woman. I got her under control."

"I don't doubt that, Viper." He called me by the nickname I'd earned because of the V-shaped scar on my left cheek.

"Remind them that the last three were not as valuable as her. This woman means something to Duran, and we can use her for an exchange if it comes to that."

"I don't think they've even considered that."

"That's why I'm in charge here with boots on the ground, and they're sitting in their offices having inane conversations about interfering in shit they know nothing about."

He chuckled. "True."

"Give me some space, and I'll make this work."

"Roger that."

"Over and out." I slammed the phone down on a table. My shoulder hurt, and I now had only two and a half hours to sleep before an important date with a perplexing woman who was part saucy T-Rex, part lost kitten.

Chapter 5 Don't Take

After two hours of light sleep, I removed my bandage and checked my wound. London had patched it up with his usual accuracy and finesse. The bullet bisected the middle of the bone frog tattoo I'd had done for a fallen brother years ago. Now the frog would have a slash across the middle. Seemed appropriate considering how many brothers I'd lost since then. If I added a tat for every one of them, I'd be covered in frogs from head to toe.

I wolfed down some coffee and a protein bar and entered the room with my rifle at my side.

Jade's eyes were ringed with dark gray bags. The woman was asleep in the bed. "I tried to get her talking, but nada."

"Okay. You're off duty."

She nodded and slid past me. I closed the door and assumed guard position against the wall.

Before waking the woman, I took the time to get a good look at her.

Her dark auburn hair, parted in the middle, fell past her shoulders. Her arched eyebrows were perfectly shaped and long nails were painted fire-engine red. Jade had allowed her to shower, and with the makeup washed off, she appeared much younger than I had initially thought. Too young to be having an affair with Ruben Duran. He was in his fifties and she could've been half that. She looked so vulnerable and innocent lying there.

The sheet wrapped around her long legs and rested on her flat belly. She'd changed from her fancy blouse into a simple brown tee that clung to a pair of really nice tits. Her refined looks didn't match with the venom I knew she could spit. She also looked nothing like any of Ruben Duran's soldiers, male or female. So how had she learned to fire a rifle and fight like a hellcat? Time to wake her up and unravel the mystery of this woman. Actually, no. As London said, it didn't matter. All that was important was if she could lead me to my brother.

I stepped toward the bed and cleared my throat. She didn't move, so I tapped her ankle with my fingertips. Before I could lift my hand, she came to life and her entire body seized up. Her foot jutted out from under the sheet and smacked the forearm of my bad arm, sending a jolt of pain radiating from the fresh wound.

She scrambled up to the top of the bed, back against the headboard, knees bent, balancing with her toes and fingertips on the mattress. Her long hair fell forward and swayed in front of her chest.

I stood still at the end of the bed. What game was she playing? Was she trying to throw me off so she could attempt an escape?

Her partially open eyes stared past me into the void. "Gollby schnok." She mumbled what sounded like gibberish. She repeated the phrase. "Goluboy schenok."

I recognized the words as Russian and stepped back. Why the fuck was she speaking Russian? The country hadn't even crossed my mind in the list of possible places of origin for her. I assumed she was Colombian or possibly American with an accent I couldn't place. It didn't occur to me at all that she might be Russian. Once again, this woman was full of surprises.

"Goluboy schenok," she said more clearly, her voice growing more agitated and shaky.

Maybe she was simply having a nightmare in Russian, but people generally dreamed in their native tongue.

"Goluboy schenok?" I replied quietly in Russian. I'd been in Colombia so long, I'd almost forgotten the words, but I grew up in Alaska with a Russian mother, and I'd had selective interactions with the Russian military as a SEAL. I wasn't fluent in Russian, but it came back to me quickly. Goluboy schenok translated to light blue puppy.

"Ne brat!" She screamed *do not take* and tucked her arms in like she was protecting something.

I drew my sidearm and held it ready in case this was all a complicated ruse to get the best of me.

"Don't take the puppy?" I asked in Russian.

She paused and her gaze rolled over me. I don't know if she saw me or not but her face crumbled. Her upper teeth pulled on her lower lip as she dropped to the bed and curled up in a fetal ball. "Please don't take." Her shoulders heaved like she was sobbing.

Well, shit. This nightmare, if it was in fact a nightmare and not an act, had reduced the hellcat to lost kitten. I felt an urge to go to her and embrace her, get her talking, but I stayed away. "I won't take," I said firmly in Russian.

"You always do." She heaved a sigh and sniffled. Her crying ceased, her body stilled, and she passed out cold.

Whoa. What just happened?

I'd witnessed a night terror. It wasn't an act. It appeared very real, and she was genuinely exhibiting fear over some kind of traumatic event regarding a blue puppy. Perhaps my threats earlier brought her other fears to the forefront. No matter what caused it, she'd inadvertently given me the best gift any interrogator could ask for. Her deepest fear and the source of her nightmares.

It would be cruel to use this information against her. Too bad I had no conscience or sense of obligation to this woman. My loyalties lay with my brother and the mission. Any debility on her part I was obligated to exploit to the maximum extent.

Chapter 6 Shelter

I stepped out of the room and locked the door. Jade was in the kitchen watching the drops fall into the coffee pot. "I got something, and I need your help."

"Sure." She poured two cups, handing one to me. "What's up?"

"She was having a nightmare."

"Yeah?"

"And she spoke."

"Always good."

"In Russian."

She sucked in a breath, and her wide brown eyes gazed at me over her coffee mug. "Interesting. Thought for sure she was Colombian."

"Me too."

"Could she be a spy?"

It bothered me that Jade went straight there, but it was an automatic reaction many people had when they heard about a mysterious Russian woman. "Not all Russian women are spies."

"True. Carry on, then. Your thoughts?"

I trusted Jade and her insight, so I blew off my annoyance with her knee-jerk reaction. "I was looking at her just now while she slept."

Her eyes narrowed.

"Don't read anything into it. I was cataloging her features. She's pretty but young. Too young for him."

"Mmm. In over her head?"

"Possibly."

"So what did she say in her sleep?"

I walked over to our communications center and wrote *goluboy schenok* on a piece of paper, spelling it out phonetically having never learned to spell or write in Russian. "I think it means light blue puppy."

She booted up her laptop and entered her security credentials.

The first search of the words turned up a cartoon about a blue puppy. She read the summary out loud. "The 1976 Soviet film featured a puppy who was born with a strange blue coat. He was ostracized for being different."

"You think she was dreaming of a cartoon made twenty years before she was born?"

She kept reading and searching. "The word goluboy came to be associated with the slang word for gay."

"So she could have some subconscious issues with growing up gay in Russia?"

"She's the blue puppy?"

"That's a stretch for a dream. She was animated. Terrified. She said, 'do not take him. Do not take.' When I said I wouldn't, she said, 'you always do.'"

"Hmm. Maybe she meant a real puppy?"

"What are some common dog breeds in Russia?"

We browsed through info on Russian breeds when my eyes caught on a striking image of a pack of blue dogs in the snow. She saw it too and read the headline. "Chemicals at an abandoned factory turn stray dogs' coats blue."

"Could she have lived by one of these factories?" I asked.

"Look at this. In Moscow, street dogs ride the metro and beg for food. Part of the culture. They aren't blue, but there are thousands of them." She scrolled through pages of metro dogs in Moscow.

Her nightmare was starting to make sense. "Is it possible she took in a blue dog as a child and her parents got rid of it?"

"Seems more likely than there being some tie-in to the slang word for gay." Jade shrugged.

"What breed are those strays?" I leaned down to get a closer look.

"They look like true mutts. Medium size."

"There are dogs like that in the streets here too. Are there any shelters?"

She did a quick search. "This one appears to be open. They're overwhelmed with abandoned animals."

My thoughts wandered from the fate of the dogs to the fate of my brother. Were they treating Teague like a dog? Were they torturing him day and night?

The image of his suffering and pain struck me like kryptonite. I doubled forward as it filled my lungs with smoke and turned my muscles to mud. No. I couldn't let the grief consume me. We had to find him and the woman held the key. I knew it. She was smart and the only one with intimate access to Duran. She had to know something.

"You with me, Viper?" Jade's words pulled me out of the quagmire I was sinking into.

I cleared my throat and straightened my spine. Back to work then. Step by step. "She's strong," I said to Jade, my voice shaking ever so slightly.

"Yep. She hasn't given us anything yet. Did you notice she didn't ask us why we'd captured her?"

"That means she knows why. If we can break through somehow..."

She was nodding and following along with my train of thought. "I'm a pretty tough chick, and these dogs make me misty-eyed."

I chuckled because Jade had been in many harrowing situations and never shed a tear. She was a lot more than a tough chick. She was a brave warrior and a good fighter.

"I wish I could help them all." She clicked through more pictures. "If I was a child and rescued a dog and someone took it from me, I'd be scarred for life." She peered up at me over her shoulder, a glimmer of mischief in her eyes.

"So we get her a puppy, let her bond with it, and threaten to take it if she doesn't cooperate." It was unconventional to say the least but also not uncommon to find someone's Achilles' heel and play it. She just had a unique weakness. "Do you think it needs to be blue?"

"No. Wouldn't matter to me."

I browsed the images of the Russian dogs again. "This could work."

"If it does, it's brilliant." Jade grinned and wrote an address on a slip of paper for me. "Start at a shelter, but you could probably walk down the street and find a stray puppy."

"True. Shouldn't be difficult. I'll take Magnum." He interacted with the locals seamlessly. His Spanish was also better than mine. "We'll be back ASAP. Let her sleep for now. If she wakes, feed her but don't question her until we return."

"Got it. She asked for clothes, toiletries, and a pencil and paper. Need your approval on those."

"Go ahead. The more you give, the more we can take away, including the puppy. I'll put Talon on her while you're out shopping. Then you're off duty to catch some shuteye."

"Roger that."

As I gathered my gear, a sense of hope replaced the smoke and mud. We had a unique advantage against a worthy adversary. If I had to manipulate her with an animal, I'd do it.

I thought of my first dog. My loyal Malamute, Siku, was my only friend in the chaos of my younger years. It broke my heart when he'd died. I'd never admit it to another soul, but giving her a dog would satisfy old wounds in me. Maybe for her too. Could it be that the shattered remnants of the boy I used to be wanted to soothe her tears and take away her nightmares? Maybe I hadn't lost every shred of compassion in my combat-weary soul.

Enough of that kind of thinking. I shook it off and headed out to find Magnum.

We were on a mission to fetch a puppy.

Chapter 7 True Evil

Skyler/Misha

The guard who'd said his name was Talon handed me a plate with rice, plantains, and flatbread.

"Thank you." I drank the water and ate all the food because I didn't know when they would start depriving me of it.

Earlier, Jade had brought me clothes and personal care items, but I didn't get too comfortable. I knew it was all a huge act to get me to cooperate, and the real interrogation would start soon.

I'd just finished up the rice when my enemy entered the room. Talon left without a word, which wasn't a surprise since he hadn't said anything the entire time he was guarding me.

As the door closed, the man set a box down next to the door. The box most likely contained his favorite torture implements. A whip, knives, maybe a taser and mace.

A tremor of fear tingled my spine. He was here to make good on his threats. Hopefully it didn't take too long before he kept his promise to kill me.

He stepped toward the bed, and his hand reached out. I turned my head and braced.

I opened my eyes and he was frozen above me, reaching for the plate of food I'd finished eating.

His gaze assessed me, his brow pulling together in question. "Did you think I was going to strike you?"

I didn't answer and looked away. The strike would come eventually.

"I wasn't going to hit you." He dropped the tray on the floor by the box. "Come sit at the end of the bed." He pulled the chair closer and sat down facing me. He waited, but I didn't move. "Sit at the end of the bed so we can talk."

I stayed put and didn't respond.

"All right." He stood and walked over to me.

I flinched when he grabbed my upper arm and hauled me over to the end of the bed. I made myself as heavy as possible and forced him to lift my dead weight. The man plopped me down at the end of the bed.

"I'm going to give you one more chance then things are gonna get ugly. What's your name?"

I avoided his gaze and stared down at the carpet.

"Now I'd like to call you something besides Eat Shit and Die, so give me a name."

I shook my head. He'd get nothing.

A ruffling sound came from the box and drew both our attention. Something was moving in there. He glanced over his shoulder and his lips twisted. He enjoyed this. Bastard.

"All right. I was hoping I wouldn't need to use this, but you've left me no choice."

Oh no. He had something alive in there. Was it a snake? If he had a snake, I'd crumble. Or a tarantula. That would be the end of me. I was deadly afraid of all creepy crawlers, but especially tarantulas. I just couldn't stand the thought of them touching my skin.

With a deep wicked smirk on his face, he reached down and lifted something out of the box.

I had to blink several times to focus on it. The entire scene didn't make any sense. He didn't extract pliers or spiders from the box. No. His massive hands held a scruffy curled little ball with tiny legs dangling.

The cutest puppy I'd ever seen.

He had a pointed snout, triangular upright ears with black tufts at the tips, and paws much too big for his stout little body. Instantly, I melted into a pile of mush. My mouth dropped open, and my trembling fingers covered my lips. I couldn't hide my truly visceral reaction to seeing a puppy. Here, of all places!

He was so absolutely beautiful.

Quickly, dread replaced my warm reaction to the animal. What was his plan? Oh no. He could torture me all he wanted, but he would not hurt a puppy. That would be beyond all realms of decency. No one had ever tortured an animal to get to me, and I doubted I could withstand it.

"You will not hurt that puppy," I warned.

"What's your name?" he replied as he drew the puppy to his chest and squeezed it. He squealed and squiggled in his grasp.

No, no, no. I couldn't bear this. "Please, do not hurt the puppy."

"Tell me your name."

He left me no choice. I had to give him something to save the animal. "Skyler Perez," I blurted out.

He lifted his chin. "Ah. Progress. Now what's your real name?"

"What's your name?" I retorted.

"Viper," he answered without hesitation.

"Is that your real name?" I asked.

"Nope."

"Then until you tell me yours, you can call me Skyler." I held my breath and pressed my lips together. Please don't hurt the dog.

"Would you like to hold the puppy, Skyler?" He raised it up, just out of my reach.

God, I was so weak. "Yes." I exhaled. I was a failure. But the puppy was completely adorable and innocent in all of this. He was just a sweet little babe. He didn't know the difference between Russia and Colombia. All he wanted was to be loved.

"You can hold the puppy for a bit." He placed it in my lap, and my hands eagerly grabbed him. I thought I might die from the incredible rush of warmth. My heart embraced every soft inch of this precious life. He was just born, fresh from his mother's teat, needing only to be loved and nurtured, but he was helpless and dependent on us to do the right thing for him. If we neglected him, he would die. If we cared for him, he would live.

"Now, tell me about your relationship with Ruben Duran, and I'll let you hold the puppy as long as you like."

I glared up at him. "You are evil. Truly evil."

"Trust me. You have yet to see a glimpse of the evil I'm capable of."

I narrowed my eyes, trying to figure him out. He'd gone relatively easy on me. Both times we'd had physical contact, he'd held back and didn't harm me permanently. Still, I was sure I'd not yet seen the worst of this man.

"Tell me how you know Ruben Duran."

"No."

"Then I'll take the puppy back." He reached for it, and I twisted away to protect it. "No."

"Tell me how you know Duran or say goodbye to the puppy." He grinned, but there was true warning in his tone. He wasn't bluffing.

I pressed my chin to the puppy's head. His fur warmed my cold skin. "I am a whore," I whispered.

The man who said his name was Viper didn't move. He remained silent and focused on me like I'd short circuited him again.

While he rebooted, I caressed the puppy. I held it to my chest. It wiggled and licked my shoulder. I loved this puppy so much.

He exhaled and wiped his palm over his face.

I wasn't sure but it seemed like a veil lifted in his eyes. The ice cold indestructible wall between us melted infinitesimally. I could swear I saw a glimmer of humanity there. Was I getting to him somehow?

He looked at me for the first time like he saw the real me. Not as a stranger but more like an old lover or a long-lost friend. I was sure I'd never met him before, but an ethereal connection passed between us in that moment.

No. It couldn't be. I was losing hold of my sensibilities. Of course he didn't feel connected to me. He was probably reveling in my total failure. I'd broken for a puppy. I'd potentially given up my life for this puppy, and I'd do it again. I'd be killed for talking to Viper, but I didn't care. As long as this puppy could lead a long happy life, I'd give anything.

"Is someone forcing you to have sex for money?" he asked quietly, and I looked up at him.

That explained the warmth in his eyes. Pity. He felt sorry for me. To me it was normal. Of course someone forced me to have sex with Duran. I'd never do it of my own free will. It wasn't for the money though. It was for the power and control. Not mine, but the power the Agency wanted to have over him.

"No."

"Are you saying you choose to be a whore, as you called yourself?"

"I'm not saying that either. I answered your question. I get to keep the puppy."

As he stood, I clutched the puppy tighter. He turned to leave the room with his head down like he had to get away from me quickly. The door lock clicked behind him. As soon as he was gone, I raised the puppy and pressed his warm belly to my cheek.

My escape plan would now have to include this puppy because I would never leave him behind.

Chapter 8 Rapport

Vander

I came out of her room and passed by Axel, Magnum, and London on my way to find Jade. Why in the hell did she bring her makeup? The woman was distracting enough without it. Now her glossy pink lips and outlined eyes had me imagining her looking up at me while sucking my cock, and that did not make me a good interrogator. It made me a giant walking dick.

I didn't find Jade, so I came back to the common area with the guys.

"How did the interrogation-by-puppy technique work out?" Axel laughed and leaned back into the couch like he was ready to hear a confession.

"Good." He was expecting me to admit failure, but I'd say the puppy won big. "She's using the alias Skyler Perez, and she's a sex trafficking victim."

He sat forward and his mouth gaped open. "You got all that by bringing her a stray dog?"

I shrugged. "It worked. She reacted instantly when she saw it. Told me her name and said she was a whore for Duran."

"And why are you out here right now and not in there asking her what she knows about Steel?" Magnum asked a fair question.

I walked away from the door as if the physical distance would lessen the problem. "I don't think she knows anything. She's not one of his soldiers or a girlfriend with influence. She's useless to us. I'm so sick of this dead-end shit. I'm done with her. Let's release her and go after Duran directly."

"Hold up." Magnum stared at me until I stopped pacing and made eye contact with him. "Her story doesn't jive with the mad gun skills."

"Or the guards. Why did he have four guards on a hooker?" Axel asked.

"She's been trained." Magnum looked from me to Axel.

"She lied to you," Axel said to me. "We have to keep the Russian spy possibility on the table."

"It's possible, but I don't think she's lying. I agree there's more going on here." Damn. This woman was extremely vexing.

"I think we should keep up with the interrogations." Jade walked into the room, and we all looked up at her.

"You gave her makeup?" I blurted out what I had intended to ask her about in private.

She stopped in her tracks, and her lips quirked. "You approved clothes and amenities. Remember?"

"You said toiletries. Not makeup."

"My role is to make her feel comfortable. I can tell you many women, not all, but a good majority of them, don't feel comfortable without at least some makeup. It's a little mascara and lip balm. Not worth mentioning."

I grumbled and turned away but couldn't argue with her logic without confessing her beauty rattled me.

"She knows something," Jade continued. "The ones who are harder to solve always come up with the most valuable intel."

Jade's intuition usually panned out to be accurate, but she'd had some misses too. With this one, I didn't know what to think.

"I gave her the puppy and she gave me an alias and told me she's a sex worker. She implied it wasn't willingly, but I didn't get the details."

"Wow."

"I agree. It's too soon to give up. I'll keep working on her, but we do it my way. No more puppies."

Jade shook her head. "I say we stick with the building rapport campaign. It'll take time. I know the process is frustrating, but we're good at this."

Frustrated did not begin to cover the excruciating pain messing around with this woman was causing me. "Physical threats work. I don't do rapport."

"You just did. The puppy got us the sex worker thing and the alias. Even if she's lying, she's talking. Let's keep at it." She took a chair next to Axel.

"I'm out of patience with her. What if all we find out is she doesn't know anything? My brother's life is at stake. If we threaten her, she'll spill fast. If she doesn't know anything, we didn't waste any time."

"The puppy interrogation technique must continue for the sake of the mission," Axel said. "You're close. Don't give up now."

I grunted. I hated this idea, but they were right. The best way to get through to her was rapport and the puppy.

"I'd be happy to go in there and build rapport with her." Magnum raised his hand.

"No. We'll do it. Let's go." I tilted my head toward Jade.

"Just you, big boy." Jade waved me off. "You triggered the nightmare. You delivered the puppy and got the name and the whole thing. I got nothing. This is all you." She paused and tapped her chin. "But here's the secret. You need to give something of yourself to her to establish trust. You can determine what that entails, but don't hold back on this one."

I looked to the ceiling and then my boots. I wanted to argue longer, but we'd be wasting more time. I was making progress with the woman and I had to build rapport, stick it out, and worst of all, give something of myself. Ugh. I made my way back to her door.

"Try cuddling the puppy," Axel teased. "Women love that."

I stopped and glared at him. "I'm gonna fuck your mother, Axel."

"Yeah? I already fucked your sister."

"That's bullshit."

"Yeah, man. It's bullshit. Lighten up."

"Nothing light about this. We have to find Steel before it's too late."

Chapter 9 Vander's Promise

"Hello, Skyler." I entered the room, keeping my voice pleasant and casual despite the growing barb of discomfort in my chest.

She scurried closer to the puppy in the corner where he was licking her plate clean. She'd placed a cup with water and spread some toilet paper out on the floor.

"Talk to me, and we'll get him bowls for food and water. He needs litter pads too."

"He needs walks outside," she snapped back.

"Then start talking." I sat down in the chair by the door. "How'd you meet Ruben Duran?"

"I don't know him." She sat on the floor near the cup of water and petted the puppy.

"He had four guards on you."

"Guards that you killed."

"The fourth one is dead because of you. Start talking or the pup goes next." None of that was true.

She growled and shot me with her death stare. As much as I enjoyed the way her eyes lit up when she glared at me, it wasn't the best way to build rapport. I needed to approach this differently according to my team. "So you cared about the guards? Why didn't you save the fourth man when you had a chance?"

"They were strangers. I didn't want them killed because of me, but I won't give up my life for one of them either."

"So you think if you tell me what I want to know right now that you'll be killed?"

"Yes."

"And who would kill you? Duran?"

She didn't answer.

"Your pimp?"

She continued to focus on the puppy and ignore my questions.

"Me? If you talk to me, I wouldn't be the one killing you. In fact, if you help me, I'll provide you protection from anyone that would try to hurt you."

She looked up at me with one eyebrow raised. I'd changed my tune, and she was right to question me.

"I assure you, I'm not the bad guy. You may have gotten yourself wrapped up with men like Duran or whoever is controlling you, but you're with me now, and you're safe. So whatever situation you were in, it could end right here." Her eyes brightened like I'd seen a few times before. She liked the idea of change. "I could make it stop, but I need you to tell me everything. How you met Duran, what did he say to you, how'd you learn to operate a weapon, why was he having you guarded?"

She chewed her lower lip and it took all I had to ignore it. Her movements all seemed so overtly sexual, but that could also be my sex-deprived brain after being downrange for so long. "Isn't that what you want? To be protected by someone you can trust?"

"I cannot trust you and you cannot protect me."

"Ahh. You underestimate me and my team. We can protect you. No matter who is threatening you. We're stronger than them."

She laughed without humor. "You overestimate yourself."

I shrugged. "I don't think so. Haven't met an opponent to best us yet, and we've been together a long time."

"How long?"

I thought about what Jade had said. *You might have to give a little of yourself.* And while I knew it was a risk, I felt it was worth it to earn this woman's trust. "Ten years with most of the operators on this team. Fifteen with a few of them."

"That's a long time in your line of work."

"I'm good. You can trust me. Now tell me where you're from."

She pressed her mouth into a thin line. Her lips were getting a lot of action, but not doing a lot of talking.

All right. Time to fess up. "I'm from Alaska. Snows like a bat outta hell there."

And for the first time, she broke a barely there grin. There it was. The beginning of the thin thread of rapport.

I continued. "I'm gonna tell you about me, and then you're gonna tell me all about you. Okay?"

She shook her head but I ignored her. "I'm the oldest of a bunch of kids. My dad was Alaska Creole, which is a mix of Native American and Russian, and my mother was a Russian gypsy." I let that float in the air for a second. Her eyes widened briefly before she looked away. I'd hit a nerve, I just needed to tap into it. "If there is such a thing as white trash in Alaska, we were it."

That got her eyes back on me. So if sharing was working, sharing I would do. "My dad was a mean drunk. Total asshole. I protected my family the best I could. Until the day he beat my sister so badly, she almost died. So I killed him."

She gasped. "You killed your father?"

"I was protecting my sister."

"Oh." She swallowed and smoothed her hair down the back of her neck.

"Now, if you were my sister, and I found out someone was forcing you to sell your body for sex, I'd hunt that person down and kill him too."

When her shoulders slumped forward, I knew I'd broken through, but I had to keep chipping away at her. "If you were my sister and sweet like you are, I'd demand every man treat you like royalty and not a whore because you look like a god-damn beauty queen to me."

Her mouth gaped open as she listened. When I paused, she looked down at the puppy.

"Maybe you have someone like that who fought for you and failed. Your parents, your sister, your brother? Because I can't imagine anyone could love you and allow you to be Duran's whore or anyone's whore. And I can't imagine a person could be part of your life and not love you."

She lowered her head into her hands. "Please stop."

I gave her a minute and then spoke low and measured. "One of my brothers is missing, and I believe Ruben Duran knows where he is, so I need you to think about your brother or your sister and tell me if Ruben had one of them. Maybe he was holding them captive in a prison somewhere, and I knew where it was, wouldn't you want me to tell you?"

"I know nothing about what you're talking about." The words scratched from her throat like sandpaper. I'd struck all the right notes and played them perfectly. I wasn't lying either. She'd see through any lies. Being honest could come back to bite me, but I didn't care anymore. Whatever it took, I'd do.

"Now it's your turn to share. Why a blue puppy?"

Her breath stuttered. "What blue puppy?"

"Goluboy schenok. What's it mean to you?"

She attempted to hide her reaction by keeping her face blank, but her eyes were her tell. The pupils grew large when she was surprised.

"Are you Russian?"

She didn't move, but her pupils flared again.

"Was there a blue puppy in your childhood?"

She had turned to stone. The puppy squealed and squirmed out of her tightening grasp. "How? How did you know this?"

"You spoke in your sleep."

"In Russian?"

"Yes. So I've told you my background and how I can protect you. Now you tell me your real name and how a Russian girl came to be guarded by a Colombian drug lord."

She stayed quiet, pressing her lips together and refusing to make eye contact.

"Did you have a blue puppy in Russia?"

She glanced at the dog and turned to me with opaque eyes. She was trying to hide from me, but failing. Her reaction was too strong to mask.

"And someone took him from you?"

"Yes." Her demeanor had changed. The sultry mystery she'd been putting off disappeared, and she'd turned into a lost child. Very similar to the kitten she was during her nightmare.

"This broke your heart?"

"Yes."

"What else did they take from you?" I stood and approached her slowly.

Her eyes followed me but she didn't pull away. "Everything."

"Your parents?"

She nodded. "My brother, like yours, was nearly taken from me too."

When I was within a few feet, I kneeled and waited for her to look in my eyes. "Then you know how important it is for me to find him and rescue him."

"I understand."

When I touched her arm, she didn't flinch. I ran my fingertips gently from her shoulder to elbow and she shivered. "Tell me where I can find him. You're safe and protected. No one will hurt you."

She looked down at my hand on her elbow. "You can't promise that."

I gave her arm a small squeeze. Not hard. Just enough to emphasize my words. "I can. There is no one who can keep you safer than me. Not in the entire world."

She inhaled a deep breath and let it out slowly. "Duran told me he had an American prisoner. He didn't say where he was holding him. He planned to use him to negotiate with the United States."

That was it. The first chance of him even being alive and in Duran's custody.

"Did Duran ever mention another city where he was lodging?"

She shook her head.

"Did Duran ever take you anywhere to have sex?"

"No."

"Did he take you out to dinner?"

"No. He said the American was alive. He planned to demand a ransom. That's all. He didn't give me any clues as to where he might be."

"Thank you. I can't tell you how much it means to me to know my brother could be alive."

"Will you release me now?"

"No."

"No?"

"Now, I'll protect you."

"Oh." She seemed truly shocked and tongue-tied. Had no one ever offered to protect her before?

"Let's take him out for a walk."

"What?"

"You said he needs a walk outside. Let's take him. It's guarded and safe."

"Okay." She still seemed rattled and out of it. She rose slowly and walked on fragile legs.

I opened the door and kept my grip on her arm as we entered the room where Magnum, Axel, London, and Jade were still sitting. All eyes came to us and the puppy she carried.

"We're gonna need some dog food, bowls, a leash, and a bed."

Axel stared at me in shock. "We're keeping it?"

"Yeah." I glanced at Jade, and her lips were tight holding back a smirk. "We're keeping him." I drew my weapon with my free hand and guided Skyler and the puppy to the front door. "We're taking him out to take a piss."

Magnum and Axel leaned back in their chairs, looking at me like I'd gone off the deep end, but I was doing what they'd asked. Building rapport. They shouldn't be so shocked.

We walked out into the courtyard. "Let him go."

She released him onto a small patch of nearly dead grass with an empty flower bed around the perimeter. He wobbled around in a circle and peed on the concrete sidewalk. She picked him up and put him on the grass. "Here, kroshka. Do it here." Kroshka meant crumb or little one in Russian. She kneeled down to watch him, and as I looked at her, I found myself wanting to know more about her.

Beneath her beauty and innocence, deep turmoil brewed and festered like a wound. The stiff awkwardness in her shoulders, and the lack of eye contact made her claim of being a prostitute seem so legitimate. When she stood up and looked at me, she inhaled and pulled her shoulders back. "Thank you," she said quietly but confidently, defiance back in her tone.

"What was the name of your dog when you were little?"

"I named him Blue."

"In English?"

"Yes. I learned English as a first language. I prefer it. I've always felt more affinity for America than Russia."

"Really. And why was he blue?"

"They thought he'd rolled in chemicals. It would have worn off eventually. I washed him many times and it didn't get any lighter. I think he ate something that turned his fur blue, and I was worried it would poison him. I was going to help him."

"And who took him from you?"

"I can't say."

The puppy had dropped a tiny load in the grass.

"You should name him Blue."

She picked him up and held him to her chest. "Yes."

"Let's get Blue inside and settled for the night. I'll make sure he has bowls, food, and whatever else he needs by tomorrow."

We walked back inside together. Whaddya know? This rapport thing wasn't so hard after all.

Chapter 10 I See You

Misha

Sergei pounded my face endlessly. I couldn't fight back and was forced to take blow after blow to my cheek until my skin felt like it would fall from the bones. "I'm sorry. Whatever I did, I'm sorry."

He turned from me and started running away with a scalpel in his hand. He ran straight to Kiri, who was just a boy wearing play clothes. He didn't see Sergei coming for him.

"No. No!" I struggled to fight, but my arms were encased in concrete.

"Shh. It's okay." A deep male voice cooed on the other side of a wall.

I opened my eyes to muscular, masculine arms around me. Not forcing me down, not restraining me, but offering comfort. Loose enough I could break away if I chose it, but I didn't want to leave this warm fuzzy oasis.

When was the last time a man had held me like this? Never. Not even my father when I was a child.

But this man who called himself Viper, who could easily hurt or kill me, was behind me in the bed, his back against the wall, his arms over my shoulders, wrapped around my waist, pulling me into his chest.

His voice rumbled and we jostled as he leaned forward to whisper in my ear. "You're safe. Just a dream. Blue's sleeping here next to you."

I looked around and found the puppy on a round pillow at the foot of my bed. Being held captive by strangers shouldn't be this pleasurable, but it was the happiest I'd ever been, and Viper was the main reason.

"Another night terror about goluboy schenok?" His tone held that twist of kindness that fooled me into thinking he cared about me. Of course he didn't. He simply wanted info from me, and I was his hostage.

"Yes." I lied because I couldn't explain to him that I had many nightmares. My lost puppy was only one of them. "I'm fine now. You can let me go." I leaned forward but his arms tightened.

"You're still shaking."

I hadn't noticed before but my pulse was pounding. "Really. I'm fine."

"Let's give it another minute to make sure it's passed."

"All right." Who was I to argue?

We sat like that in silence for a while. My heart rate returned to normal, but my body was freaking out. I couldn't be that close to him without being affected. My neck heated and my legs tingled.

He must've felt it too because we both grew stiff and slowly inched out of the embrace.

"I'm sorry," I said.

"Why are you sorry?"

"I must look ridiculous having these nightmares about dogs." In my peripheral vision, I saw two weapons by the door. He'd removed them before he approached me. Made himself vulnerable so he could comfort me.

"Not ridiculous. Human. A human who's been traumatized. I wish I could have a conversation with whoever took that puppy from you."

"No. That wouldn't be good."

"You deserve better than that. You were an innocent child. Who would take that from you and force you into the life you have now?"

"Your mother didn't tell you these things?" He'd said his mother was a gypsy. They led very difficult and poor lives in Russia.

"I know. She was a mail-order bride."

He'd said before that his father was an abusive drunk, so his mother came here to escape poverty and ended up in a worse predicament. "Is she why you're pretending to care about me? Not because you want information from me?"

"I'm not pretending to care, and it has nothing to do with my mother or the information I need from you."

"You expect me to believe that? What does it matter to you if I was treated unfairly?"

"It wasn't just unfair. It was cruel. I care if that happens to any woman."

I threw up my arms and tried to be angry at him, but it was weak. "Then go out and save all the women of the world because there are many of them."

"But you're the one in front of me right now." He remained calm and didn't take the bait to fight.

"And I could be gone by tomorrow. Don't put yourself at risk for me. It's not worth the consequences." I grabbed Blue and walked away from the bed, turning my back on Viper and the crazy things he was saying.

"I'll be the judge of that."

He sat quietly for a long time. I couldn't help but look back at him and take him in. His long legs and boots took up half of the bed. He kept his other foot on the floor, probably a strategic move if he had to get up quickly.

The space between his legs looked so tempting. I would love to give into the urge to be cuddled by him again, but I knew it wasn't safe despite what he'd said.

I couldn't trust him at all, and yet he spoke so matter-of-factly he'd almost convinced me it was true. He didn't need to hold me when I had a nightmare to achieve his goal of extracting information from me. The warm glow in his eyes couldn't be faked. We were playing a dangerous game and both of us seemed to be getting pulled into it.

"I have nightmares too." His soft voice broke the long, tense silence.

"You do?"

"Yep."

"What are your nightmares like? I can't imagine you being afraid of anything."

"I'm running. Always running in the wrong direction. The people I love are behind me, and I'm running the other way. Never fast enough. Bullets flying overhead, bombs exploding all around. I'm always running to save them but never get there."

"That sounds awful."

"I care about you because I had dogs as a kid too. It was rough when they died or I had to leave them behind."

"What kind?"

"I had a Malamute, some Huskies. They pulled the sled when we went out hunting."

The image of a young man in the snow with his pet Malamute pulling a sled filled my mind. I bet he took good care of his sled dogs too. He was that kind of person.

"I loved sledding. I always wanted to be a musher. I wanted that puppy so I could train him and we could escape into the wilderness."

"I actually did that." He chuckled.

"You did?"

"We'd run from my dad sometimes when he was on a bender. Camped in the Alaska Bush for weeks."

I'd never camped in the snow, but I'd spent plenty of time in sub-zero temps. The weak succumbed easily to the cold. Only the strong survived.

"That's so dangerous."

"Not so bad if you're equipped."

"You seem like a man who is well-equipped." I smirked, trying to bring some light to a midnight dark situation with no possible path to rectification.

"You have no idea how well-equipped I am."

Was he flirting with me? "I don't doubt that." Well, lo and behold. The evil demon holding me hostage had a humorous side. Amazing.

"I see you," he said with his warm brown eyes on me, all humor gone as quickly as it came. My stomach dropped. He could expose me and I couldn't trust him, but the way he pinned me with his eyes, I believed him. He saw me and it felt terrifyingly good.

"You don't know me," I whispered back.

"I know you want out. You want me to help you. You're just scared."

"You don't know all of that."

"I'm telling you I see you. Not what you're presenting on the outside. I see the real you. Someone no one else has ever seen."

I looked down. "You see what I want you to see."

"Sometimes it takes a mirror to see yourself clearly, and you're reflecting all kinds of shit at me I don't want to look at or talk about either. But I've seen her twice now. A young girl who had her life torn apart. She's never been loved in the way she should. She still wants it. She needs it. It's not too late, but it's up to you to take her by the hand and guide her there."

"What kind of shit?"

"What?"

"What don't you want to look at about yourself?"

He grinned and gazed over my shoulder for a moment. When his eyes came back to mine, he asked me an unanswerable question. "Tell me your real name."

I shook my head. "She doesn't exist anymore."

"She does and she's tired of hiding. Let her come out to play. She's a hellcat."

"Ha! You think my true self is a hellcat?" He'd really fallen for the ruse if that's what he thought of me.

"Part hellcat part kitten."

"That may be true, but..."

"I hear you saying you won't let me help you with your situation and that's what it all comes down to. You have to want it and fight for it. Take that beautiful girl inside by the hand and lead her to a safe place where she can finally get what she needs even if it seems impossible."

"You speak in platitudes and daydreams. I'm surprised for such a tactical man that you allow your thoughts to wander like this. I may be safe in here, but if we walk out the door, we have to face the truth."

"The truth is you're making excuses. Change that. Make solutions."

I nodded but didn't say anything. His mottos wouldn't erase the debt I owed to the Agency. They killed my mother, my father. Sergei wouldn't hesitate to kill me and my brother if he even suspected I had plans to defect.

"My real name's Vander."

I gasped. His unsolicited announcements always stunned me.

"Now tell me yours."

I was so tempted to tell him everything and trust him, but I knew it could never work out. The Agency didn't let their property leave without paying a heavy price. "Just call me Skyler. Please."

He stood and walked over to the door but stopped and looked back at me with half-lidded eyes. "One last thing, Skyler."

"Hmm?"

"Blue will be a good sled dog. He's got what it takes, and I can see determination in his eyes."

"You can?"

"Yep. The same determination I see in yours."

"I'm sure he will."

"Will what?"

"Be a good sled dog someday. He just needs some time to realize his power."

"Yeah." He picked up his weapons, walked out, and locked the door behind him.

And as I sat alone in the empty room, I had the distinct feeling my life had changed. I didn't know how yet, but a critical milestone had just passed between us. More than his real name, which I loved to hear, something else.

We'd shared. We'd connected, and it wasn't in my imagination this time. He'd said it out loud. He saw me and cared about me.

He wasn't the automaton I'd first thought he was. Despite the threats he made in the beginning, he seemed like a solid man, a complicated man, obviously a sexy man. Maybe even a man I could love, if I were capable of it.

I allowed myself a fraction of time to entertain the fantasy that I was safe in his arms, his ripped body behind me, supporting me, protecting me, turning me on, teasing me. It would only ever be a dream, but it was mine to keep. In my head, no one would find out I'd fallen for the enemy.

Chapter 11 Say Your Name

Vander

Catching a quick break while she slept, I closed my eyes and leaned back in the chair by her door, resting my head on the wall.

I thought of Teague. He went by Steel, but he'd always be Teague to me. He could be alive. That thought kept me from crumbling over in pain. Duran had an American prisoner who could be my brother, and for the first time in a long time, I had hope that we were close to finding him.

Thanks to her. I'd told her too much already but it was worth the risk. Beyond that, I enjoyed diving into her mind, her world, her fears, her desires. I didn't lie to her either. I saw her true self hidden under all her camouflage.

The difference between us was I could also envision a future for her, but her mind blocked out those ideas. She held herself back. Self-sabotage of the worst kind. I've been known to engage in some self-sabotage of my own, so I couldn't throw stones. We spoke the same language, and not just Russian.

The sheets rustled and the springs creaked. Through thin slits of my barely open eyes, I watched her slip out of the bed and peel off her clothes.

My heart rate slowed, and I switched to stealth predator mode. Alert on the inside, unmoving on the outside.

She approached me cautiously like I was an IED that could explode in her path. I absolutely was as volatile as a bomb, and she was right to move slowly. Of course, she shouldn't be moving at all considering her situation.

She walked over to where I was sitting and stood between my legs. The only coverage she had was a flimsy lace bra that looked about two sizes too small for her gorgeous tits and an equally lacy and just as dangerous pair of underwear.

Jade really needed to stop treating the hostages like spa guests. Cotton underwear would've been more than generous and a lot less lethal, but this woman would probably tempt my resolve no matter what she wore.

She was a knockout by every standard. Big eyes, full lips, tan skin, round tits, curvy hips, legs that never ended. Movie star beauty. The opposite of me and my scarred face and crooked nose. Everything about her turned me on, but the reality was she was my captive and much too close.

I struck like the Viper I truly was, grabbing her wrists with a tight grip she couldn't escape. She gasped and pulled back, but I held firm, forcing her to stay close to me.

We stared at each other for a long second. She was likely calculating the risks just as I was doing.

I drew her hands behind her back which brought her tits right below my face. "Careful, Kroshka." The word for "little one" slipped out. She'd used it earlier for Blue, and I thought it fit her too. She had a lot of lost puppy in her.

"I'm no little one." The sultry vixen voice had returned along with her sexy-as-hell confidence.

"To me you are."

She arched her back and breathed out as her tits brushed my chin. The hellcat was horny and wanted to play.

Damn. My dick was already rock hard. I didn't touch women when I was deployed. I didn't jack off. In the field, you survive. Your physical needs are eating and sleeping. Keeping your weapon close and ready. Paying any attention to your dick could get you killed, but I knew she couldn't overpower me and I couldn't summon the strength to turn her away. I'd be giving up so much. The heat coming off her, the long hair cascading over her incredible tits, all of it right in front of me like a buffet.

The stitches of the injury pulled tight as I removed my weapons and placed them on a table out of her reach.

She craned her neck, bending her head forward to tempt her lips next to mine, begging me to kiss her. I looked at her pouty lips but kept my distance. Even though my restraint was hanging by a tattered thread, I'd shown her no external response that would encourage her. This was all her.

I tugged her arms back as a warning. "Don't do this, Kroshka."

"I'm not doing anything," she said as she climbed up on my lap and straddled my hips. I wasn't encouraging her, but I also wasn't stopping her.

I ground my teeth together. "You're playing with dynamite, woman." All my muscles were strung tight like a slingshot ready to discharge.

She pulled forward and managed to press her lips to my jaw in a soft, hot kiss. Her lips were every bit as luscious as I'd imagined.

I looked to the ceiling and took a deep breath. "Damn."

At the first sign I'd let slip that she was affecting me, she grinned and rolled her core over my dick through the fabric between us.

On her next pass, she found the line of my shaft through my pants and drilled in on it. The contact caused my balls to draw up and my dick to twitch. My cock did not give a shit if this was wrong and dangerous. It wanted to dive into her tight wet heat.

No. I had to keep my cool.

That's when her scent hit me. Feminine and sweet. It would be my undoing, that scent.

She let out a ragged sigh and rubbed her hot core up and down on my cock again. "It's huge." She panted and let out a tiny whimper.

Shit. Fuck. She was getting herself off with the friction. If she didn't stop, I'd lose the tenuous hold I had on my control. If she did stop, I'd lose control too. That was it. I would not survive this.

"Open your pants for me. It feels so good and so big. I want to see it." Her velvet voice triggered another surge of lust to my cock. Lethal. This woman was absolutely lethal.

"Tell me your real name." My strained words stuck in my throat with the mammoth effort it took to hold back.

"No," she said coyly, like she had no clue she had just climbed up on a viper's lap and was about to get bitten by his fangs.

"Say your name and I'll open my pants for you. Give you everything you need." I spoke through clenched teeth, swallowing hard with the effort of forcing my body to do the opposite of what it craved.

"No," she repeated mischievously as she writhed on my dick.

Through the fog of tits and pussy on my brain, I struggled to focus on her motivation. What did she really want from me right now? Not just my cock. What else was working behind those beautiful eyes? "C'mon, you're desperate for it. You want me to fuck the real you. You want me to say your real name when my cock strokes your sweet pussy. You want me to moan it when I lose control and explode inside you." As much as I wanted to, I had no intention of fucking her. I'd say what it took to get her name.

She mewled, her hips still rocking mine in the cruelest of tortures. The fabric of my pants started to get wet from her exuberant oscillations. I should tie her hands back so my fingers would be free to fuck all that wetness coming from her.

No. I absolutely could not take it that far.

"Say your name," I gritted out.

Her hair fell over her eyes as she shook her head. So sexy and distracting. I forced myself to focus on the goal. Fucking her senseless.

No. No. The goal was to extract information. Jesus. I'd totally lost all restraint, and all she'd done was ride me over my clothes.

"You're showing me the real you right now. I can see her. She's fucking beautiful. Tell me who she really is."

She chewed her lip, and I jutted my chin to suck it out of her teeth. I growled and nipped her bottom lip as I pulled it taut and released it. "Tell me your real name." I tugged her arms back, creating more space between us and threatening to end this if she didn't comply. It would be hard as hell to tear her off me right now so hopefully this was the last time I had to ask. "What's your name?"

"Misha," she finally whispered.

Thank God. "Misha." Her name rolled off my tongue like it belonged there. "Misha," I said again with reverence. "Feels good to hear me say it. Doesn't it?"

Her shoulders relaxed, and her arms went limp. "Yes."

My hellcat had submitted. We were done. I had her real name. I should've stopped, but no man, even one of my strength and countenance, could turn down the woman sitting on my lap especially after she'd given control over to me exactly as I'd wanted. She'd put her trust in me, and I was going to reward her for it.

With one hand, I worked open my pants and yanked my rock hard dick out. I placed my thumb under her jaw and fingers on her neck, forcing her to look up. "Just this. No more." Somehow my addled brain had negotiated an imaginary limit that made this all okay.

"Let me take off my panties."

Her whispered plea hit me dead-center in the balls. I groaned through it. "No. Just this," I rasped.

"Just this," she agreed reticently.

"Then take it." God, yes. Take it soon before I explode.

She arched her hips and landed her sweet pussy on the tip of my shaft. Holy shit. So hot, wet, soft, sexy. The fabric of her panties was a soaked non-existent barrier between our skin.

Someone please stop me from impaling this woman on my dick.

She wiggled like a dancer, grinding until I felt it slip between her folds and rub against her clit.

The chair shook beneath us, and I steadied it with my feet flat on the floor. She bit her lip and doubled down like she was peeling a cucumber.

"That's it. Take what you need."

I sat there mesmerized watching her get herself off while she jacked me with her soaking wet pussy.

She inched closer, forcing me to tighten my grip on her wrists. "Just this."

She whimpered and gave up her efforts to bring our torsos together. The rhythm of her thrusts sped up like she was bringing it home.

Her breath hitched, and she pulled one hand free. I captured it again, but not before her open mouth landed on my jaw and hot puffs of air blew against my skin as she bucked against me, her needy pussy pulsing endlessly on my aching cock as she came. I was hypnotized by her mouth, her breath, her scent. I'd have given anything to be balls deep in her when she came hard like that.

My chest heaved and my breath stuttered. My hard cock was dripping and straining to get inside her. What the hell just happened? I could not form a coherent thought except we could be fucking on the bed in five seconds if I just gave in.

No. God, no. I'd told her just this, and I had to keep my word even if my dick turned blue and imploded.

Okay. Maybe I could give her one small kiss on the lips, but nothing more. When I allowed her to close the distance, she went wild, her lips pulling and sucking, begging me to throw her on the bed and finish what she'd started.

Okay. Enough. I had to end this.

With Herculean effort, I managed to tug her off me. I walked her over to the bed and placed her in it on her back before I let go of her wrists. Despite being free for the first time, she didn't attack. Instead she bent her knees and spread her legs, her fingers coming between them to drag through her own wetness under her panties. Her eyes found mine and the devilish hellcat teased me by licking her fingers. "Hmm. Delicious," she said in Russian.

I should take this hard cock and jam it into those lips and force her to suck me off till she gagged.

No. No. God, no. I'd already let this go much too far. "No," I finally said out loud what I'd been trying to say the entire time. I tucked my rock hard weeping dick into my pants and zipped up. I marched to my weapons and repeated it. "No." For her or for me, I didn't know.

Luckily, the door slammed closed behind me before she could say or do anything else to bring me to my knees. At least I made it out alive.

Chapter 12 I Feel You

The lock rumbled as I struggled with it, fighting to tamp down the brewing storm she'd created with her voodoo rain dance in there.

"Fuck." My fist collided with the wall with a loud crunch. "Fuck." It stung, but I punched it a few more times. It didn't ease the chaos. I'd risked my team, my brother, the mission, everything. So stupid. I'd get away with it for now. No telling what the long term consequences might be.

"Go ahead and bone her already." Magnum's voice came from the entry to the kitchen.

"I can't."

"Why the hell not?"

I paced the room looking for something else to hit.

How the hell did I lose my mind like that? I prided myself on my restraint and cool headedness. Shit. "A few days ago I was willing to put this woman through her paces. Now, I would kill a fucker who tried to hurt her."

"So go back in and give her the beans."

"She's a weakness."

If she was manipulating me, having sex with her would ruin everything. Never let your guard down. No matter how tempting. The basics of tactical training.

"She's actually pretty harmless. Whether you guys play a game of Mr. Wobbly hides his helmet or not, doesn't change the mission, doesn't change the risk, nobody has to know."

I was way too frustrated to laugh at his stupid comments. "Is this what you tell yourself every time you screw someone while we're working?"

"Has it ever backfired?" He leaned forward and raised his eyebrows. Cocky asshole.

"C'mon. Remember Sheila?" That woman wreaked havoc on his personal life for a long time.

"No. I mean has it ever jeopardized our safety or hurt a mission? No. Never. Go bake the potato." He pulled his wallet out of his pocket and held up a Magnum large-sized condom.

"Are you serious?"

"You know what *is* a weakness? Blue balls and a raging boner. That is a weakness. Go glaze the donut. I won't tell anyone."

Man, I had to be far gone if Magnum's food analogies were making sense.

"Fine." I swiped the condom. "Take custody of my weapons." I handed him my rifle and sidearm.

I was about to ask him for another condom when he spoke first. "Watch your back though. Pretty bitches like her can turn around and stab a knife in your ass."

Oh no he didn't. Not now. I pushed up into his face and he flinched. "She is not one of your bitches. You don't know jack about her, so don't say stupid shit like that."

"You getting attached to this girl, Viper?" He made a tsk tsk sound that pissed me right the fuck off. "Bad idea."

"Of course not."

He stared at me for a second before backing off.

I did an about face and marched back into her room. I didn't have time to duke it out with Magnum. She was hot, wet, and ready for me, and my dick couldn't wait a second longer.

When I entered the room, she pulled up on her elbows and her mouth opened to speak, but nothing came out because I had shut the door and made it to her in a few steps. My lips sealed hers and silenced whatever she was going to say.

Her hands rose toward my face, but I stopped her and held her wrists tight to the headboard.

"Let me touch you," she begged.

Despite what I'd said to Magnum, the girl was still a risk, and I knew better than to let her get her hands on me. One twist of my head and she'd break my neck. "You take what I give you. I give you what you need. You take it all because it's good, and you might never get this kind of good again. So take it and enjoy it."

I ripped the wet lace panties off her and took in her naked pussy. Pink, glistening, a small patch of thin curly dark hair. Fucking beautiful. I wanted to taste it, but I couldn't restrain her and eat her at the same time. I growled and ripped open the condom with my teeth. These were supposed to be extra large, but they fit me snug and barely hit the base of my cock.

"Look at me, Misha."

I hovered over her, and when I got her eyes, we were linked up in an inexplicable way. "I see you."

"I see you too, Vander. I do."

That hit me hard, and I closed my eyes to combat the rush it created in my gut.

When I slid inside her, it wasn't just physical ecstasy. I was filling a need in her, and she was filling something in me. We couldn't name it, but old bullet wounds were being repaired. She moaned loud and long, and I hadn't even moved yet.

After giving her a second to adjust, I let loose. I went as slow as I could for three thrusts, but then I was dust. I couldn't take another second without ramming into her fast.

She groaned, and I swiveled my hips to make maximum contact with her sensitive bud. It wasn't just rutting. She'd had enough of that in her life. I knew how to make it good for her and me at the same time. It was a sensual dance played to music only we could hear.

I pummeled her hard, lifting her knee up over my shoulder. Her head lodged up with each thrust. Driving deeper and deeper.

It was so fucking intense I thought I'd self combust. Finally, finally, when I thought I couldn't wait another second, she gasped and threw her head back, mouth open. Her tight walls constricted even tighter around my dick as a long strangled moan rang from her throat.

My spine tingled and my stomach clenched, my balls drawing up. "Misha, yes. Misha."

I said her name to make it clear. *I see you. I feel you. I'm here with you.*

And then I let go too. Holy shit, it felt incredible to release into her, giving her what she needed while taking at the same time. It washed over me like the headwall of a flood clearing out tons of debris. I needed this so much more than I knew. I drew it out as long as I could before the condom started to slip. I held it on and pulled out.

She was exultant, like she'd captured the king. Smiling, eyes closed, her leg came off my shoulder to wrap around my hip like an embrace.

She pulled her head up and tugged my ear lobe with her front teeth. "Thank you," she said in Russian.

Again my gut twisted. This woman tore me up inside.

I let go of her wrists and walked to the bathroom to dispose of the condom. She showed no signs or plans to attack. In fact, she was languid and loose, lying limp in the bed.

"I warned you, Kroshka," I said as I came back from the bathroom and zipped up my pants.

"Mmm. Warn me again," she said lazily.

"No. Just this."

"Okay." She grinned.

My "just this" was worth shit.

I leaned down in the bed and gave her a final kiss. "You won this time. You got me."

"I wasn't trying to get you."

"But I got you too."

"Hmm?"

"You revealed yourself to me."

"Well, yes." She smirked and peered down at her tits, which were tinged an enticing blush from the friction of our fucking.

"I did more than see you. I felt your true nature. The real you."

She got quiet and looked to the side.

My fingers tipped her chin back toward me. "She's staggeringly beautiful. Truly sublime."

I kissed her cheek and stood up. As I walked to the door, a strong magnetic pull drew me back to the bed. I wanted to hold her and protect her from nightmares, but this time I found the strength to stop myself.

Just this. This is all we had and could ever have. "Goodnight, my Kroshka."

We'd face the fallout of this in the morning. It happened. I blew it. Was it worth it?

Fuck yeah.

Chapter 13 Mercy

Talon had just gotten off duty and was unloading in his cage, the wooden storage areas we'd constructed in the common area.

I noticed my rifle and sidearm stacked in my cage. Magnum's version of taking custody was dropping them and leaving.

Talon and I worked silently side-by-side checking our weapons and organizing gear. His silence bothered me sometimes, but right now the quiet provided a welcome buffer for the turbulence in my head.

Misha. Sweet as sin. Hot as hell. Challenging and submissive. Each golden crumb of info she gave up made me want to keep working her until she revealed every last bit about herself. She needed so much more of what I'd given her. I wanted to run right back in there and take her again, condom or not, until she begged for mercy, but I couldn't risk it. I'd seen this happen a million times. A guy follows his dick and gets it chopped off.

"I'm out."

Talon stilled and angled his chin toward me, waiting for me to explain my random outburst.

"You take over with the detainee. I'm out. I won't be talking to her."

Once again Talon's silence was coming in handy. Giving her up would torture me, but it was for the best.

After he chewed on it for a second, he tipped his chin and returned to his work. I trusted him with her. If it couldn't be me, I wanted Talon there. If she had another nightmare, he wouldn't comfort her. He'd stand strong and stoic like I should've done.

They told me to build rapport, and I fucking took it too far. I put us all at risk, especially my brother, but my team, even Misha could be hurt because of my actions.

I'd still be there behind the scenes watching every development, but I couldn't trust myself with her again.

"Viper!" Jade's voice called from the command center we'd set up in a separate room. "Got something."

Talon stopped and looked at me. We both dropped our gear and hustled over to Jade. "What'd you get?"

Magnum and Axel entered the room and walked over to us, quickly picking up on the tension. "CIA made contact with Duran. He wants to exchange her for Steel."

Holy shit. This is what we'd been waiting for. "Terms?"

Our two other tech specialists, Shadow and Locke, sat opposite her on their own laptops, typing furiously too.

She clicked around as decoded messages flew by on her screen.

"I got it," Shadow said. "Cartagena Country Club."

"When?"

Each question took them what felt like forever to answer. "It's all coded. We have to decode and make sure we got it right," Locke said.

Jade nodded at him. "I agree. It looks like midnight tomorrow night. Colombia time."

That gave us less than twenty-four hours to prep her.

"Proof of life?" I asked. Please, God. Let him be alive.

They all went quiet and clicked around for a long time. "Stand by. So much going on at once." Shadow sounded as stressed as we all were.

"There's audio." Jade squinted at a small file attached to some code.

"Audio of what?"

All three of them stopped typing at the same time. Jade's face drained of color. Shadow and Locke looked at me first then away.

"What is it?"

"Nothing. There's audio. They're trying to authenticate it." Jade shook her head as she worked.

"Audio? Of my brother?"

She didn't answer.

"Play it. I can authenticate it in seconds."

She shared doubtful looks with Locke and Shadow. "It's not confirmed it's him."

"I will confirm if it's him. Play the damn audio."

Jade disconnected her earpiece and turned up the volume. She looked away from me like she didn't want to watch my face.

The sound from her speaker instantly paralyzed me like a stingray's barb had pierced my heart. The agonized long wail was no doubt my brother. I'd know it anywhere. I couldn't breathe. I forced myself to stay standing. Be strong. Call on my training.

A series of loud strikes and painful grunts followed. They were hitting him with a flat piece of wood. Be strong.

"Please. Mercy."

Yes, that was my brother.

Another long howl and my knees hit the floor. I was not strong. I couldn't listen for another second to my brother's endless torture. The scalding pain, the bitter guilt. My fault. It was because of me he was suffering. I never should've sent him on the assignment. Too dangerous. I had faith in him. God, the weight of it crushed me like a tank had fallen on me and smashed me into the sand.

My legs brought me back to my feet and I walked through what felt like a tunnel to my cage to pick up my sidearm. I couldn't hear their warnings as I left the building. I didn't listen to anyone. I needed to kill someone.

I found myself standing outside in the small range we had set up. I could see it all. My brother tied up, begging for his life. Ruben Duran standing above him with a two-by-four. He needed to die. I took aim and fired my weapon between his eyes. I drained the entire magazine into his body. He was just a sack of sand on the ground, but damn, I wanted to kill him. I would give my life to take my brother's place.

The weapon was empty so I could not punish myself for what I'd caused, but if I died, who would save him? My fault. I did this to him. My mistake. I was supposed to protect him and I blew it. We'd never recover from this. We'd never be the same. My nightmare had come to life. My brother needed me and I kept running the wrong way.

Chapter 14 Compromised

Misha

The door opened suddenly and I quickly covered myself. The one Vander had called Magnum stood in the doorway and glanced at my body before turning his attention to Blue, who had shot up to greet him. He was equally tall but thinner than Vander and much more personable based on the small grin his mouth had quirked up into. From his dark skin and rich brown head of hair, he could've been South American or Spanish, but with his thick beard, I couldn't really tell much about his face.

"I need you to take the dog out right now." He grabbed the leash and hooked it on Blue's collar.

"Okay."

I finished dressing and made sure not to show any outward sign of my disappointment that Vander hadn't returned to walk the dog with me. As we walked through the common area, I sensed an odd stiffness in the air. Something had happened. Jade and two other men stood with their arms crossed and legs wide as they peered out a window.

Magnum led me to the back of the house instead of the front, where I had walked Blue in the courtyard before. As Magnum opened the door, my heart jumped into my throat.

Vander, my big strong machine, lay collapsed on his knees in the dirt, his gun hanging loosely from his fingers.

Magnum handed me the leash and Blue pulled toward Vander. I held him back as I took it in fully.

His shoulders hung forward as he stared down at the dirt. Blue scratched and clawed to get closer, but I gave him a tug

80

and he got distracted by a scent on a blade of grass. I looked up at Magnum for permission and he nodded before he left me alone with Vander.

I approached him slowly, but he didn't move. It was the most frightening thing to see the man who had been nothing but strong every time I'd seen him literally on his knees, not weeping, but lost.

"Vander?" I whispered. "Are you okay?"

Blue sniffed him from behind and he still didn't move. I came in front of him and let Blue lick his face. He slowly unfroze and stared down at Blue with blank eyes. I placed my palm flat on his face and tried to raise his head. He was a stone statue. "What happened?"

His eyes tracked Blue as he sniffed around us.

"Is it your brother?" If his brother was dead, it would kill him. "Did something happen to your brother?"

I let Blue go run around the yard and dropped to my knees in front of him. "Talk to me, Van."

His hand swung out and landed on my hip. His fingers dug in and he tugged me toward him. His back slowly uncurled as he pulled me into an embrace.

"Is he dead?" I whispered and wrapped my arms around his shoulders. Our torsos lined up, the firm muscles of his chest pressing against my breasts and our tummies bumping together.

"No," he whispered back and finally raised his eyes to look at me. I couldn't stand the vacant pain I saw there. "Much worse."

"I have you, Van. I have you right here."

"It's my fault."

"It's not."

"I should've protected him."

"You can't protect him from everything."

"I can."

"No one can."

His other hand came up and pulled my hair into a knot at the base of my neck as his forehead fell onto my shoulder.

We held each other like ice sculptures until the gravel dug into my knees and the sun burned my shoulders.

Slowly. Ever so incrementally, his muscles loosened, his hands started to gently caress my back, and he raised his head. The storm had passed.

Blue sniffed his face and Vander reached out to pet him like he'd just realized he was there. "Hey, boy."

Now that I had him back, I needed to get him talking. "Tell me about your brother."

"Duran has him." His voice scraped against his throat. "They're... torturing him." He dropped his head again.

I placed my palms on his cheeks and pressed them together until he looked up. "I'm here. I have you right here. He's alive?"

"Yes."

"Then we have to go get him." I don't know why I included myself in "we" but it felt right.

"They want you in exchange." A dark shadow fell over his face.

"Then they get me."

He was quiet for a long time. He'd tormented himself over this, but he didn't need to.

"Your team over there is watching us right now. They need their leader to be strong. Your brother needs you to command this mission. If Duran wants me, I'm fine with that."

He shook his head, not willing to accept the impossible choice of me versus his brother. In my mind, there was no doubt his love for his brother far outweighed any glimmer of passion and connection we'd shared in the short time we'd known each other.

"You got this. How many hostage exchanges have you been involved with?"

"A few." His lips quirked up on one side.

"Me too," I whispered in his ear. I was revealing myself, but he'd laid himself bare before me already.

His eyes widened as he assessed me, likely putting the pieces together. He'd slept with a Russian agent.

He nodded and wiped his palm over his face as he stood up, offering me a hand to help me up. "I want you to go in wired."

"No. Too risky. Just get him out clean."

"You go in wired to make sure you're safe. We get my brother out. If you're in danger, we come for you too."

"No."

"No debate." He squeezed my hand.

"I won't be in danger."

"We'll make sure of it."

"Duran won't hurt me. He loves me."

His neck stiffened and he closed his eyes like he was warding off pain. "I'm compromised," he said in a whisper.

"What?"

"Talon will take over prepping you for the exchange." He stepped back and let go of my hand.

"Okay." That hurt. He was saying he was compromised by me.

"I'll oversee it. From a distance. I can't talk to you." He struggled with the words, but we both knew it was what needed to happen.

"Okay."

"You'll be safe."

"I'm not worried about me anymore."

"We can do this. We get him out first and make sure you're safe."

"Okay."

"Gonna kiss you goodbye now. Won't have another chance."

"Okay."

He stepped up to me and wrapped his big hands behind my back. They warmed my skin and supported my spine. He pressed his lips to mine and I could taste the longing there. Pain and desire flared deep in my belly. It had only been an hour since we'd shared our intimate moments in the bed and it felt like we'd come so far.

I deepened the kiss and whimpered. It would agonize me to leave him, but he needed his brother back alive. If I had to let him go so he could have that, I'd do it. We were never meant to be anyway. I had to return to my assignment with Duran, and he had a life to live with his family and his brother. A life that didn't include me.

"Bye, Kroshka." His lips quirked, but his eyes didn't wrinkle or smile with it.

"Bye, Viper."

After a small press of his lips to my forehead, he turned and left me standing alone with Blue.

Inside, a huge boulder fell on my heart and smashed it to pebbles. He was so close and so far away. Like everyone in my life, ephemeral and fleeting. But Vander wasn't like anyone else. He was the only one who had truly seen me and for that I was thankful.

Magnum came out through the back door and squinted into the sun. "He done with his business?"

"Who? Oh, Blue? Yes, he's done."

"Let's go."

I took Blue's leash and Magnum followed us inside. How much did Magnum see and know about what just happened between me and Vander? Probably everything.

Chapter 15 The Handoff

Jade finished installing the listening device in my necklace and checked once more to make sure it wasn't visible. She clicked on a tablet and smiled. "Tracker's active."

The tracker was actually inserted in my vagina in a tampon-like case. I'd never worn one like that before, but it was a novel idea. They'd have to invade my cavity to get it out, and I wasn't going to let anyone get that close to me.

"Will Viper be at the exchange?" If he wanted to invade my cavity, however, I'd be totally open to it.

"Yes."

I gulped down a huge sip of water. I hadn't seen Vander since our last conversation in the backyard. He'd kept true to his word and installed Talon as my security guard. Talon didn't speak to me the entire time he stood watch. I spoke to him a few times, but he remained unshakably cold, unfriendly, and expressionless. Similar to the way Vander was in the beginning, but also the complete opposite of the Vander I'd come to know.

"He told me to remind you that you can't tell anyone anything about what happened here. Don't mention our names. Never tell anyone in Russia that we agreed to a prisoner exchange with Colombia. If you tell anyone, you risk all our lives."

"He said to tell me that? Well, tell him I had no intention of sharing confidential intel with Duran or my associates in Russia, but please also tell him how absolutely thrilled I was that he didn't trust me to already know that." I said it straight-faced with stony eyes.

She didn't respond, but I caught her lips teasing a smile. Did no one speak back to Vander? They should start. He needed to be put in his place when his head grew too big for his pants.

"Plan A is the exchange goes off without a hitch. Plan B, if you are in any danger, we come in and extract you."

"We don't need a plan B. Ruben Duran is in love with me. He won't mess this up."

"Hmm. We'll see. He also said you keep the dog no matter what."

"He did?" I held back a sigh. At least I had Blue.

"Let's go."

I understood why Vander wasn't here himself to tell me these things. Like he said, and I'd repeated to myself the past few days, he was sticking to his promise to maintain the integrity of the mission. I would never do anything to stop him from finding his brother, but if he felt what we'd shared made him weaker, I had to accept that, even though it hurt. I didn't know what I expected him to do instead. Come to me and kiss me goodbye? He'd done that already. Pledge his love to me and beg me to stay with him forever?

No. He had a job to do and so did I. His brother's life hung on our every move, and we had to be smart and focused. For all I knew, the intimacy we'd shared and all his talk about the real me could've been subterfuge. To me, it felt like the most authentic experience I'd ever had, but he was likely doing what he needed to do to find his brother. I'd accepted that and would play my role accordingly. I was used to ignoring my personal whims anyway. This was no different. Yet again, I played the mindless pawn in someone else's chess game.

We grabbed Blue and left the compound in a caravan of cars and SUVs. Talon, Magnum, and Jade rode with me. No sign of Vander when we loaded the vehicles, but I assumed the mic was live and he could hear us. We stayed quiet on the ride over. A weird mix of anticipation and regret hung in the air.

Tonight I would say goodbye to the people I'd met a week ago. People who made me feel like I'd known them a long time. I'd never see them again, and they wouldn't think twice about me in the future. This was always my lot, never making lasting ties, always moving on to the next mission.

The lead car stopped at the top of a slope deep inside the Cartagena Country Club. The hills of the golf course were shrouded in shadows. A low fog loomed in the valleys, and the place felt like an abandoned cemetery. My heart thumped so loud I'd imagine Vander could hear it through the earpiece.

Magnum and Talon left the vehicle first and waited for me to climb out with Blue in my arms. I stood between them as Jade stepped up behind me. Everyone was heavily armed except me. The jeans, T-shirt, and puffy mylar jacket Jade had given me wouldn't protect me if gunfire was exchanged. I felt vulnerable. The only thing in my arms was a small bag of belongings and a tiny puppy.

In the scant light, I could make out a line of men standing between two pickup trucks about fifty yards away. Ruben's men wouldn't kill me unless he gave the order, and if he still loved me, I was relatively safe. Still, anything could happen.

A conspicuous form emerged from the lead car in our caravan. Broad massive shoulders and tall long legs strode toward us with confidence. So intimidating in his flack vest, helmet, and gear. He was not messing around. Whatever confidence he'd doubted the last time I saw him, he'd found it and ampli-fied it ten-fold tonight. He was the real-deal. A true-to-life su-perhero not to be messed with. I'd grown up around spies and assassins, but Vander had a special kind of swagger that would make their blood run cold.

Now I knew why I'd seduced him. He was magnificent. I was lucky to have had my time with him.

As I gawked, he walked up to me and made eye contact. He didn't blink or nod, but his eyes locked on mine for a brief sec-ond, and I felt that look in my bones.

He stepped in front of me and shielded me with his body. The vulnerability I felt instantly disappeared once he became the impenetrable wall in front of me. For the first time, some-one had stood in front of me when I faced the firing line. No one else, my brother, my father, no one I'd worked with had ever walked up and shielded me from anything. The cowards always ran and pointed fingers in my direction, leaving me to fight by myself. That was fine. I didn't need them, but it sure felt good to have Vander and his competent team around me right now.

A few more of Vander's guys fell in line beside us. "Let's move." With those two words and a short pause, the team start-ed forward like one synchronized body, sweeping me up in their momentum and shuttling me closer to the meeting spot. The only sound was the rustling of their gear.

As we approached the line of men opposite us, I could make out Ruben wearing a black peacoat, his hands in his pockets. He wasn't armed, but all the men around him held ri-fles at the ready. His gaze lingered on Blue for a moment then he looked at me directly. He stood straight and combed back his hair. He was either excited to see me again or nervous.

They had a tall man with them who had a sack over his face.

"Remove the face covering," Vander called in Spanish.

"Send Skyler to me first," Ruben replied.

"That's not how this works."

"It works how I say it does. Now if you don't want him dead, send the woman first."

I clutched Blue to my chest. We could do this. We would survive whatever happened. I stepped out around Vander, and he glanced down at me. Tension rolled off him, but he didn't need to worry. I knew what I was doing. I nodded and walked toward the center of the field. Vander and Magnum followed behind me.

In the center, Ruben's soldiers took my arms. Vander and Magnum took hold of the other prisoner. They walked backward and we walked forward. Goodbye, Viper.

Ruben's men urgently pushed me to the door of a black SUV. I tripped and dropped Blue but recovered with my hands on the seat.

"Hurry, hurry." Ruben climbed in behind me.

"What's wrong?" I asked as I gathered Blue again.

"Nothing." Ruben gritted his teeth.

"Did something go wrong?"

"No," he snapped.

Looking out the back window of the vehicle, I watched Vander and his men take off the hood of the man they'd exchanged. When they removed the covering, they didn't embrace or celebrate. Instead they turned and started shouting. "Is that his brother?"

"Yes."

He was lying. I could tell by the agitation in his voice, the nervous clenching of his fists, and the cautious grin underneath it all. "Why'd you do that? You promised him his brother." Vander would be crushed.

He took my hand. "I have you now. That's all that matters."

"Do you know what they'll do to you for this? Those guys are deadly."

"They won't retaliate. They still need the brother."

Ruben had deceived Vander and his team. What kind of man would do that? A vile dishonest man. That's what Ruben was.

How could I fix this? Vander was listening. Ruben implied he still had his brother but didn't bring him to the exchange. He was holding him hostage somewhere. I needed to find out where.

How could I use my position with Ruben to lead them to Vander's brother? Asking him directly where he was holding him would raise too much suspicion. I needed to think of something because I couldn't ride off with Ruben and leave Vander and his men behind with nothing to show for it.

What if Ruben became angry with me? He'd have to become so enraged he'd force me to go to prison. Possibly the same prison where they were holding Vander's brother.

"Don't worry. You're fine now." Ruben took my hand and rubbed it as if to warm me up.

It was a long shot because Ruben might not bring me to the same prison. He might kill me here and dump my body by the side of the road for being a traitor, but it was worth the small chance I could still help Vander.

Based on what I knew of Ruben, he prided himself on his control of the people around him. No one dared to speak ill of him. This idea could work. I'd be putting my life at risk for him, but my heart compelled me to take the chance.

"I'm sorry, Ruben. I told them everything."

His hands stopped moving and his gaze came up to mine, his crazed eyes looking at me sideways. "You did what?"

Yes, now that I'd started, I was committed to this. It could work. If not, I had nothing to lose. "I told the Americans what I know about you."

"You... You betrayed me?" He glanced out the front window and then the back as he rose up in his seat. His hands shook and his face puffed up. "What did you tell them?"

This was good. He was getting angry. I had to keep it vague or he'd kill me now. "I told them your plans to expand your territory." In fact, Ruben had told me very little about his plans, but that didn't matter. He needed to think I'd given them juicy info. "They know everything."

Ruben bristled with rage, and it only took five seconds before he processed my words and raised his flat palm to strike my cheek.

I enjoyed the sting. It meant this was working. "Why would you do this to me after I did all this for you?" He motioned around the car, like doing a fake hostage exchange was some huge undertaking for him.

"I had to clear my conscience. I don't want to be associated with a drug dealer. Drugs cause so much destruction and pain for people."

His eyes widened, shocked at my words. Ruben lived in a bubble where shipping huge quantities of drugs was a big profit-making operation not a cancer on society that ruined lives.

"What did you tell them?"

"I won't say, but they know enough." This should anger him more because he couldn't kill me until he knew what I'd shared.

"You won't say? What the hell is wrong with you, Skyler? Stop the car." His hands twitched like he wanted to hit me again.

This was it. He was either going to kill me or pass me off to someone else to do it.

We pulled over into the gravel on the side of the road, and Ruben kicked open the back door. He pushed me hard, over his legs, until I fell out of the door. I landed on my knees in the gravel, and Blue tumbled out behind me. "She's a fucking traitor. Put her in another car. Take her to detention. Have Angel question her until we know exactly what she told the Americans."

Yes! I might end up tortured or dead, but the slim chance remained that I'd be leading Vander to his brother.

I clutched Blue's leash tight and dragged him along as the guards transferred me to another vehicle. They'd have to pry this leash from my cold, dead hands.

Ruben drove off, and I was alone with his guards who spoke quickly in Spanish, making plans to drive me to this Angel person. They made a U-turn on the road, and I looked out the back window. No one was following us. "Where are you taking me?"

"Shut up." He punched my temple, and the pain vibrated through my skull. If I passed out, I couldn't help Vander anymore, but hopefully I'd done enough. He'd know where to find me and hopefully his brother too.

Chapter 16 By His Kindness

Angel, the man who'd beaten and interrogated me for what felt like forever, tossed me into a room. It had several cots, a toilet, and a sink.

I attempted to hold up my torso, but it was pointless. I fell to the cold tile floor and sobbed. I hadn't cried through the punches and the threats, but when he poured scalding water on my back, I broke down and wailed.

The room meant the torture was over. I'd survived and reached my destination.

I managed to keep one eye open. Had I succeeded? Was this all worth it?

No. No one was in the room with me. I'd hit rock bottom. I'd sacrificed myself and my dog to find Vander's brother yet I'd ended up alone again.

When the Agency found out I'd betrayed Ruben Duran, I'd face their wrath. I'd be tortured, much worse than the boiling water today, and killed. My body would be buried in Siberia, and no one would even know I'd died.

As was my life, so shall be my death. I never existed. The blinding pain on my back surged, and my vision went black. The last thing I heard was the door opening before my cheek hit the tile.

***

My back burned like an arsonist had a picnic on it. I was lying on my stomach, face turned to the side, but not on the tile floor. I was lying on one of the cots in the room. Large boots approached me slowly. A man wearing pants with stained knees crouched down beside me.

Big brown eyes looked down on me, his brow deeply furrowed. Swollen dark bruises bubbled out above his two black eyes. Dried blood crusted to the side of his mouth. "You awake?" he asked in a deep voice, and my head spun. I knew that voice. He looked just like Vander. Had he rescued me like he said he would, or was I hallucinating?

I tried to pull my arms underneath me and turn over, but he stopped me with his hand on my shoulder.

"No. Don't move. I have wet towels on your back. You must be in horrendous pain. Try to drink some of this water." He poured a few drops into my parched mouth, and I was able to swallow it.

"Thank you," I rasped.

As I gained consciousness, it became clear I was still in the prison cell and the man with me wasn't Vander. He looked like him though, and he was caring for my burns even though he was battered and bruised himself.

It had to be his brother.

I knew him by his kindness.

My heart that had given up all hope began to pound fast. I had to think while I had the chance. Everything was groggy, but I needed to focus.

Okay. I remembered Angel had taken my necklace with the microphone at some point, but I still had the tracking device in place. Vander should still be able to find me.

We were alone in the room, but that didn't mean Duran's men weren't listening to us. I had to choose my words carefully. "Are you from Alaska?" I asked in Russian.

He blinked and his mouth dropped open. It was clear now he was a younger version of Vander. Dark lashes, beautiful brown skin, black hair, tall and muscular. Yes, I'd found him.

"Yes," he answered in Russian. "I am."

I was betting on the likelihood that none of our Colombian captors spoke Russian. "Your brother has found you," I whispered through the dry burn in my throat.

He came closer and poured more water into my mouth. "What are you saying?" His intense eyes intimidated me, but I knew that look. This was Vander's brother. His Russian wasn't as good as Vander's, but it was him without a doubt.

"It's a matter of time, but he will come for you. I know it."

"Which brother?"

"Viper." I'd forgotten he had more than one brother, and he wouldn't know which one was leading the effort to save him.

He nodded slowly. "What's your name? How do you know him?"

"Skyler. He brought me a puppy." I closed my eyes as the grief rushed through me for my dear sweet Blue.

I should've known better than to get attached because anything I loved ended up destroyed.

"A puppy?" his brother asked.

"Yes." And with my answer I felt peace. This was all worth it. For the first time in my life, I'd made a selfless decision for the sake of someone else. I could've let Ruben drive us away from that handoff and returned to my life before Vander, but I could never forgive myself for not doing all I could to help him. I took this risk and it paid off. "He'll come for me and find you. You have to stay alive until he gets here."

"Why did he buy you a puppy?"

"I think he was a stray. I can't talk about it. He died. Angel killed him."

His eyebrows drew together. "Do you speak English?" he asked in English. "You lost me in Russian."

"Yes. I speak English." It would score my heart to have to say it again, but his brother had asked about Blue, and I was obligated to answer. "Angel killed my dog."

He glanced at the closed door and then back at me. "Did you see this with your own eyes?"

"No."

He leaned close and whispered in my ear, "When we break outta here. I'll check for your dog."

"See? You are kind like him."

"My brother and I have been called a lot of things, but kind is not one of them." He chuckled under his breath, his eyes glinting like he was remembering antics with his brother.

I didn't believe him. Vander and... "What's your name?"

"Steel."

Vander and Steel were kind and compassionate, and I doubted they'd ever prove otherwise. Men of honor. The opposite of me. A woman built on lies and deceit. I didn't deserve to be among them. Maybe this whole thing was my lame attempt at being part of something virtuous. For a brief moment, I got to be the good girl who sacrificed herself for the sake of the team instead of the black widow coming in for the kill.

Steel sat on the cot next to mine for several hours as I struggled through the pain. When I moaned, he would add more water to the towel over the wound.

"When do you think they'll come?" I whispered.

"It should be quick if the conditions are right, which they never are, so I have no idea how long we'll be here." His concerned gaze moved to the towels over my back. "When we lift you, it's gonna hurt like hell."

I groaned. "I can't be carried in this condition." My top half was naked and the skin on my back was badly scalded. One touch would cause an agony of fire.

"Let's remedy that now."

He moved to my feet and grabbed the bottom of a sheet that I hadn't even realized was there. He ripped it into a long strip. "This'll hurt, but it'll make it possible to carry you out. Can you sit?"

"I can't move."

"C'mon. I know you're in pain right now, but you gotta dig deep for whatever grit you can muster."

"I cannot muster grit." That sounded like a very American phrase I'd never heard before, but I could tell from his tone and context, he wanted me to persevere. He gently and slowly forced my shoulders back and somehow, with his encouragement, I was able to clench my teeth through the pain.

I covered my naked breasts as he draped the sheet over the wet towel that was already across my back. He didn't react when I lowered my hands and exposed my front to him.

Like I thought, honorable.

I helped him by holding the sheet in place as he made two more passes.

"It's a temporary solution until we can get you proper care." His tongue came out at the side of his mouth like he was working a jigsaw puzzle as he tucked it in under my arm to fasten it.

"You're far too kind."

"Please stop saying that. Humans help other humans. It's normal."

"Not for me."

He helped me to lie on my stomach again. "Rest now and if my team arrives, I'll carry you out and look for your dog."

"Please just get yourself to safety. For your brother's sake."

He crouched in front of me and squinted as he scrutinized me. "Why do you care about us so much? What happened between you and him?"

It was such a long story. How did I break it down? What information could I trust him with? I chose my words carefully. "We became entangled because of my association with Ruben Duran. Your brother was looking for you, and he felt like I might know where you were."

"Did you?"

"No. I knew that Ruben had an American hostage and after some convincing, I told Viper that I knew this information."

"Convincing? Did he interrogate you?"

"Not anything like this. No. He didn't hurt me physically."

"Hmm. Instead he bought you a puppy?"

"Yes." It was difficult to admit my weakness aloud, but the puppy had sparked long-buried memories of my life before the Agency. When I had two parents and we found a blue dog in the alley. It was my first pet. A living thing I could love fully with all my heart and cuddle endlessly. Then that was all stripped from me so I could begin my training.

"And you told him you knew I was being held by Duran?"

"I thought it might be you. Yes."

"I still don't understand how you ended up here. What's your association with Duran?"

"I betrayed him."

"How?"

"It's complicated. Let's not discuss it."

"Oh no. We are discussing it. Spill."

I sighed and closed my eyes. "There was an exchange set up. Me for you. But Duran brought a decoy. He took me and ran before Viper and his team could do anything to stop it."

"My brother was holding you prisoner?"

"Uh, yes."

"And Duran valued you enough to do an exchange? Where does the betrayal come in?"

"I lied to him and told him that I had revealed all his secrets to the Americans because I knew it would anger him. He would arrest me and take me to prison."

"Why would you do that? You wanted to go to prison?"

I remained quiet because he was putting the pieces together on his own.

"You lied, knowing they would arrest you and possibly bring you here? You sacrificed yourself so my brother could find me?" His voice rose in pitch and volume with each word.

We weren't being careful. Hopefully no one was listening to us.

I closed my eyes. "Yes." I knew it was foolish, but I had found his brother so it was not in vain.

"That's not how hostage extraction works. You don't make yourself a prisoner too. Then you have two captives at risk. My God, woman. That was so dangerous." He stood up and walked away from me.

"It worked." I quirked my lips.

He spun and his eyes burned. "At what cost, Skyler? At what cost? Look at your back. You've been beaten. No. You shouldn't have done it. When Viper finds out..."

"He knows. He was listening."

"You were wired? Did he hear them torture you?"

"I don't know how much he heard."

"God. He must be going ballistic."

I doubted that Vander was thinking of me right now. Steel was his mission, not me. "None of that matters. He'll come for you, and you two can go home to reunite with your family."

His eyes grew darker as he spoke through gritted teeth. "We're getting you out of here, and we're gonna find the dog. Viper would want that. It's obvious you mean something to him and he means something to you."

Vander had changed my life, but I was certain I didn't mean anything to him. "It's complicated."

Steel paced away again and dragged his palms over his hair as he stared at the locked door of the room. The movement was identical to Vander when he did it.

He paused and turned stiffly toward me with one finger over his lips, his eyebrows raised.

Chapter 17 Brace For It

The pop of machine gun fire outside the door sent Steel leaping onto my back. Fire exploded on my scalded skin, and I had to roar through the pain. He lifted his chest off my back. "Sorry."

"Is it them?"

The echo of gunshots grew louder and closer then stopped.

A loud bang of something slamming into the door followed. "You in there?"

"Here!" Steel called back.

Three more thunderous strikes on the door and the entire thing flew off its hinges and landed flat on the floor.

Vander led a group of men, weapons ready. He scanned the room and moved directly toward us. "Clear."

Steel stood and turned to face his brother. "Quite the entrance, man."

The other men took up positions at the door.

Vander kept both his hands on his rifle and surveyed Steel and then me up and down. He tipped his chin at his brother then turned his gaze to my back. His forehead furrowed under his helmet.

"She has burns," Steel said. "We have to be mindful of them." Steel helped me to a sitting position as he had done before. Vander growled and cursed when the bandage made out of a sheet was exposed fully to him.

"I'll carry her," Vander announced loud and clear.

Steel held me steady and looked up at him. "She faces your front, one hand on her neck, the other below her waist."

Vander nodded but stood frozen in place, staring down at me.

"Give me your weapon." Steel held out his hand. "I'll cover you."

Vander handed him his rifle but didn't move to pick me up. God, this was awful. I was distracting them from completing their escape and reunion.

"Leave me, Vander. Get your brother to safety."

"This is gonna hurt. Brace for it, Kroshka." I didn't brace for it. I didn't hear anything except him calling me Kroshka. *Little one.* He deftly scooped me up, one arm under my butt, the other behind my neck. He held my face to his shoulder and pivoted toward the exit. "We're out."

The sheet fabric and towel scraped against my injuries as Vander carried me through the blown out door and then the front door of the building. It hurt like hell, but Steel was right. If he didn't touch the bandage, there was less pain.

We reached a helicopter and Vander called out, "London, burn injury on her back."

A man placed a blanket on a bench in the middle of the cabin. Vander carefully set me down so I sat upright. "You need to lay down?"

"No. I can sit." With all the action, the pain had somehow lessened.

The man I assumed was London approached us and examined the bandage Steel had made.

The crack and pellet of gunfire started up in the building again.

Vander and Steel were winded from running to the helicopter. They grinned at each other through heaved breaths. "We going back in?" Steel patted Vander's back.

"You up for it?" Vander asked.

"Hell yeah. Been dreaming about it."

Vander grabbed a new rifle from inside the helo and jumped out. "Be right back."

I closed my eyes and prayed they would be safe as I breathed through the pain.

"I'm going to cover you so we can remove the bandage." London placed a scratchy blanket over my shoulders and reached for the closure of the sheet. I helped him open and unwrap it.

My back stung as the towel came off and the cool air hit it. As he worked on it, I realized it wasn't my entire back that was hurt. There were two main regions. One by my shoulder and one lower on my spine.

I heard more gunfire and my heart leaped into my chest. If they were hurt now, after all we did to save Steel, it would be a catastrophe.

Before I could get too deep into the worry, they returned to the helo with the rest of the team. They filed in around me. More of them than I had seen before.

They took seats on benches and Vander sat next to me. With a thumbs up to the pilot, the helicopter took off and lifted us.

As we got higher and farther away, the men in the cabin started to take off their gear. Vander stood up and embraced his brother, their bodies pressed together.

They hugged for a long moment, gripping each other's arms and slapping each other's backs. Holding on tight and relishing their reunion.

It was noisy, but I thought I saw Vander mouth, "I'm sorry."

Steel shook his head. "Not your fault. Don't do that."

Vander nodded and let him go so he could hug Jade, Talon, and Magnum. The rest I didn't know, but they greeted Steel and welcomed him back.

The relief and joy the team felt after the successful mission filled the cabin. I let it wash over me vicariously. I wasn't part of this group, but for a second, I allowed myself a moment to share in their celebration.

"Are you hurt anywhere else?" London asked me as he finished bandaging my back and checked my eyes and arms.

"Just my back."

"I can give you something for the pain until we get you grounded."

"No. I don't want to sleep now." I wanted to enjoy every minute of this combat victory with the elite team I was pretending to be a part of.

Jade came up to me and said, "Thank you."

I didn't deserve any gratitude for this. I was the grateful one because they had rescued me. I was a stranger. They probably suspected I was a Russian agent and yet they still helped me. They could've easily left me behind.

Vander released his brother and turned to me. "You're gonna be okay, Kroshka."

"Blue..."

"No worries." Steel crouched as he moved over to us. He carried a blanket rolled into a ball. As he slowly unrolled it, my frightened puppy's ears and then his little black nose came into view. He shook his head and panted.

"Oh my God." Steel placed him in my lap, and I pulled him up against my chest. I fought the rush of tears as he licked my chin.

My puppy was alive. He'd survived so much. The magnitude of it all hit me like a train wreck. Through all the fear, loss, pain, regret, and longing my life had been. This was who I was meant to be. Part of a team of heroes who rescued the target instead of killing him, and who took the time to find a puppy in the middle of a combat zone.

The touch of Vander's hand wiping the hair from my brow forced a tear to drop from my eye.

"You're safe now. I got you."

Yes, for now, I was safe and he had me. Hook, line, and sinker.

Chapter 18 Hold My Hand

Vander

We landed at an airstrip along the southern coast of Colombia. Grady arranged a meet with a platoon from SEAL Team 7 that had been searching for Teague. The word spread quickly that Operation Strong as Steel was a success. We had recovered Teague. I had my brother back safe and alive. Special ops teams around the world were celebrating tonight.

After a short greeting at the air strip, the SEAL team escorted us to a safe house in a remote area. We'd lay low for tonight, see to any injuries, and fly out tomorrow.

I made the mistake of looking when London took off Misha's bandage. Her beautiful skin was marked with blistering red welts, but the skin wasn't broken and there was no blood.

My hands shook as I paced the room. "I feel like jumping out the window and tracking the bastard down to show the asshole what it feels like to be burned alive."

Teague was sitting back in a chair with his legs stretched out in front of him. "We got him." One of the medics had seen to his face and head injuries. Apart from the dazed look in his eyes and dilated pupils, he seemed relatively okay considering the conditions.

"We did?"

"The one upstairs where the dog was being held. Angel. We shot him."

"Is he the one who tortured you too?"

He winced and looked down. "Yeah."

"He got off too easy. We shoulda captured him and made him pay."

"No. It's cleaner this way."

He was right, but I wasn't seeing logic at this point. For the misery and torment he'd caused my brother and Misha, he should rot in purgatory forever.

"He's dead, Vander. You can't kill him again."

London finished his treatment and left Misha sleeping on her stomach. "She took the pain meds. We need to keep her well hydrated and change the dressing once a day. With some rest, she should be healed in a few weeks."

"Can she travel?" I asked.

"Resting here would be better, but if it's not safe, we can move her."

"Okay."

He looked at Teague's bruises again. "If you feel dizzy, let me know."

"I'm good."

"Glad to hear it. This whole op was FUBAR, but you're back with the team. That's all that matters."

"Yep."

London patted him on the back and left. I took a seat next to Teague at the small table by the window and glanced at Blue sleeping at the foot of Misha's bed.

"I can't believe how good it feels to see you again," I told him. "Been obsessed with this since you were captured. Two months. Never stopped looking for you."

"I knew you wouldn't."

"I hoped the entire time that knowing the teams were looking for you would help you withstand."

"It did." His eyes looked vacant and shell-shocked.

"You wanna share what went down?" For the rest of my life, I would never forget the sound of his cries for mercy.

"Not ready to discuss it yet."

Fair enough. He had a lot of processing to do first.

"When you're ready, we talk. Don't let that shit simmer because we both know what happens."

We'd lost several brothers in arms who'd taken their own lives because they couldn't cope with the memories and the chicken stew that combat hours make of your brain. The most recent one was fresh in all of our psyches.

"I won't let it simmer."

"Need you to talk to a psychiatrist. Got plenty back home and a new one who specializes in combat stress."

"I don't need that." He took a sip of water and his eyes shifted.

"It's mandatory. You need to work this out, so it doesn't eat you alive."

"You gonna talk to her too?" He peered up at me.

"No." I had to be honest with him. I didn't like to talk about this stuff either.

"You look more fatigued than me. Let's get some sleep and tackle it tomorrow. I'll take that bed." He pointed to the second double bed in the room.

"I'm in it with you."

"What about Skyler?"

"Her name's Misha. She's Russian."

"I got that much when she spoke to me in Russian. Couldn't follow it so we switched to English."

I closed my water bottle and chuckled. "You need to brush up your skills."

"No, I don't. If you get a contract in Russia, I ain't going."

"We don't have any contracts for Russia."

"Good. Now tell me about her."

She looked beautiful as she slept peacefully. Such an amazing woman. "Nothing to tell."

"Not what she said."

"What did she say?"

"She said it was complicated."

"True."

"Spill."

I took a deep breath and tried to verbalize all that had happened. "She was Duran's mistress. He visited her villa every two weeks, so we captured her and took her in for questioning. I was gonna go hard on her, but she had a nightmare, and I found out she had a weakness for dogs, so I got her a dog." I shrugged.

He nodded like he'd heard this from her. "And then?"

"Then uh, I became, uh, compromised so I withdrew, and Talon handled her until the tradeoff." I looked down at my boots.

"How did you become compromised?" He'd already picked up on it. I could hear the smile in his voice.

"Jade told me to give her something of myself." I looked up to see his grin. It was nice to make my brother laugh again.

"Oh shit. What did you give her?"

"My real first name. Told her Mom was Russian. We're from Alaska. That's it."

"No last names, birthdays, social security numbers?"

"Shut up."

"Whatever you gave her, it worked. She sacrificed herself for you."

"That was for you."

"She didn't know me. It was for you."

I shook my head. Still couldn't believe the stunt she'd pulled. "Shocked the hell outta me when I heard her tell Duran that shit. Had to listen to him hit her." I cleared my throat and my stomach roiled. "Listened to her cry when that Angel motherfucker poured scalding water on her back."

"You lose it?"

The rage burned and churned in my chest as strong now as when it was happening. "There were some broken windows while I kicked everyone's ass trying to set up the recovery in record time."

"I bet."

"She held strong. Did not give up one thing. We got in there ASAP and here you are."

"Here we are. Where do we go next?"

"I think you should visit Atlanta. You need your family right now."

"No. I mean her. Where does she go?" He angled his head toward her sleeping form.

"She goes wherever she wants." My gut pinged at the thought of saying goodbye to her.

"Just like that?"

I nodded. "London said she can travel. She's not my prisoner anymore. She's free to leave."

He stood up and walked away from the table. "She risked her life for us. We owe her more than that." I understood the frustration in his voice, but our hands were tied.

"Like what? We can't bring her in any deeper. The CIA already wanted to kill her. As of right now, they're allowing her to leave because they think she doesn't know anything. The more she finds out, the closer to death she dances. We have to cut her off now."

He stopped and looked at me with his hands on his hips. "I don't think she's a risk."

"I don't either. It's what the feds think. They're concerned about her. I want her gone and safe."

"I can hear you both." Her soft voice was muffled by her pillow.

Oh shit. We'd woken her.

"I'll call my contact and be gone in the morning," she said quietly.

"That's not necessary," Teague answered.

"I am a liability."

I walked over to her and crouched down at the side of the bed. "You're incredibly brave, Kroska." She squeezed her eyelids shut. "Look at me, please."

She slowly opened her eyes to slits.

"We're talking about your safety. You've already been through too much, and I don't want to be the one who brings you more pain."

"You can't hurt me. I'm unbreakable." One side of her mouth turned up.

"I believe you, and I've seen it in action. What you did for my brother was sheer valor, but the more you're seen with me, the more dangerous it gets. Duran is going to be looking for revenge, and the US government has you on the radar as a security risk."

"I'm good at disappearing. Like I said, I'll be gone in the morning."

I felt like a selfish bastard for not begging her to stay, but the truth was she had to go. She'd had a front-row seat to our movements, conversations, weapons. It all put her in the bullseye.

"Before I leave, can I ask you one favor?"

"Ask me anything, babe."

"Hold my hand."

That cut me deep. I wanted to hold so much more than her hand, but I took it in mine and squeezed it. She felt cold and delicate.

"Hold it while I sleep to keep the nightmares away."

"You got it."

Teague took the second bed, and I lay down next to Misha, giving her enough space to make her back comfortable, but slowly moving in until I could feel her heat buzz through my body. Everything about this woman affected me viscerally. I brought her hand to my lips. "Spakoynay nochee, malyshi." The phrase meant "Goodnight, little one," and was the title of a Russian TV show that was supposed to help kids fall asleep. She may have been too young to know about it, but my mom had played the videos for us before we went to sleep.

"That show is terrifying." Her lips curled up into a smile.

"It is." I had to chuckle because those puppets were scary as hell. "I'll just say goodnight then."

"Goodnight."

Chapter 19 The Coin

Misha

My brother Kiri waited for us at the meeting point in the parking lot of the airport. Vander followed my gaze and scrutinized him through the darkened windows of the SUV. "That your contact?"

"Yes."

"You sure you're safe with him?"

"I'll be fine."

He nodded but didn't take his eyes off my brother. The other team members stepped out of the car, but he didn't move. He was giving us some time to say goodbye.

I hadn't been alone with him since he'd held my hand while I slept. As we prepared for today, he kept his distance and didn't make eye contact, but I could sense the pending farewell weighed heavy on his mind. The words stuck in my throat. "Goodbye, Vander."

The hazy shield covering his eyes suddenly turned crystal clear. I committed it to memory, so I could sketch it later and return to this moment.

He was allowing me to see inside the vulnerable, earthly part of his soul instead of forcing me out with his perfunctory facade. He became a man with deep unmet needs, and from what I saw in his eyes, I filled in some of the divots that life had carved into his spirit. I loved that I had this effect on him, yet hated that I couldn't give him anything meaningful. I promised myself I would not break, but I forgot to say I wouldn't break him.

"It's not up to me. There are other factors in play. People who would hurt you if they knew what you've seen."

I held up a hand to stop him. "I understand and I have no regrets. This is where we are today. We have no choice. I have to go. It doesn't erase anything. I'll savor it in my memory." I would draw and sketch every moment I'd spent with Vander and his team.

His eyes scanned my face and he nodded. He tilted his head and slid his fingers into my hair at the base of my scalp. His strong hands were so capable and self-assured. Lethal and gentle. A complex contradiction of a man who stirred thoughts and emotions in me I shouldn't entertain. And yet, every time he touched me, my haunted shadow whispered in my ear, *It's possible. There has to be a way for us to be together. Find it.*

His warm lips landed on mine, rough at first and then soft and pliable. He teased mine open and our tongues clashed, my insides buzzed, and I was instantly hungry for him in the most carnal way. I couldn't say the words, but I tried to convey it all to him in the yearning of my kiss. Did he understand me, or was all of this in my head? He pulled away and wiped his lower lip like he was savoring it. "Me too."

Yes. We understood each other. The connection we'd forged would break today forever. He was just another land-scape passing by from the window of a train. I couldn't stop and enjoy a sunny day or dip my toes in a frigid lake. Why did I have to constantly say no to the things I wanted? It didn't make sense.

I centered my dizzy head and inhaled a deep breath. Time to confront the reality of my life I'd been avoiding for far too long. I picked up Blue's traveling crate and placed it on the seat between us. "Take him."

"No, Kroshka."

That would probably be the last time he would ever call me Kroshka. I'd miss him, but at least we'd shared something I think neither of us had ever experienced and never would again. "I can't have a puppy where I'm going, and I don't want anything bad to happen to him. You'll take good care of him."

He slowly gripped the handle, and his eyes simmered. He knew that if I was going somewhere I couldn't have a dog, I was being controlled. It was no secret between us, but it hurt to admit it aloud and give up my beloved puppy. I opened the door to the crate and pulled my wiggling puppy out to give him one last kiss. Saying goodbye to him and Vander felt like ripping my heart out and tossing it in a raging fire. "Bye, Blue. I love you more than you'll ever know. You be a good boy for Vander. Okay?"

He licked my face, and I forced myself to return him to the crate.

"It's time." Vander handed me my small bag of belongings and opened the door from the inside. By the time I'd climbed out, he'd left the car and come around to my side to help me out.

Three team members from another vehicle walked over to join us. Jade shook my hand. Magnum dipped his chin, and Talon did nothing. Not once did I see Talon crack a smile or even talk. The man was as still as the statue of David, yet he'd chosen to come to see me off, so I assumed that meant something.

Steel held out his arms. I stepped back at first, shocked by his offer, then I gave in and stepped into a hug. If my brother saw me embrace him, so be it. I'd explain it somehow.

Steel kept his hands on my shoulders, careful not to touch my back. We'd survived the unthinkable together, but I knew we'd both have long-lasting footprints on our souls. No matter the extent of your training, torture took it's toll. I was worried how he'd handle it all but also couldn't allow myself to care. I'd never see him again. "I hope you're able to muster grit when you need it," he said as he grinned and offered me his hand, which I thought was odd after the intimate hug.

I took it and shook it firmly. "Goodbye, Steel."

"Bye. I hope you find what you're looking for." As he said this, he pressed something metal into my palm. He locked eyes with me, tilted his head, and looked down at our joined hands. I hid my surprise and slid the coin into my pocket smoothly so my brother couldn't see.

I glanced at Vander again and memorized his face as I fought back the flood of tears wanting to escape. His strong jaw, deepset eyes, crooked nose, and the scar on his cheek. I knew I would make many sketches of his face, but it would never ease the pain of leaving him.

The walk away from Vander and his team toward my brother seemed symbolic of my entire life, always walking or running the opposite direction from where I wanted to go. Vander's nightmare was my reality.

I reached my brother and he smiled. At least I had him on the other side, if I had nothing else. Kiri embraced me quickly and took my bag. With a brief look back at my temporary "team," I turned and walked toward the terminal.

***

I kept my finger on the coin in my pocket as we boarded and gained altitude. What in the world could Vander's brother have given me when I'd never see him again? A memento of our torture? I doubted it. Once the seatbelt lights went off, Kiri finally spoke. "Tell me everything."

"Good to see you too, Kiri."

"I'm sorry. Are you okay?"

"I can't discuss." I motioned with my eyes to the people around us. We couldn't risk it.

"Where were you?" He kept up his questions even though we weren't secure. I took it to mean he cared about me and wanted to know what I'd been through. He could also be watching out for his own back making sure his rogue sister didn't get him in trouble as I had done in the past.

I leaned over and whispered in his ear, "I was kidnapped by Americans who wanted intel on a hostage. The exchange went badly, and Duran's men believed I had betrayed him."

He sucked in a breath and turned his fiery blue eyes at me. "But you didnt?"

"Of course not."

"Tell the truth."

"I am. Misunderstanding. The Americans rescued me and returned me to you. End of story." It was, in fact, the truth. I just left out the part where I risked my life to sacrifice myself for an American.

"Who was the man you embraced?"

"He is one of them. Just very friendly. Nothing else."

"Do they know you're Russian?"

"No. They think I am Skyler Perez." I chose to lie about that fact because I didn't want to share this with Kiri. It was my private adventure and of no consequence to him. The Americans wouldn't be able to find me again even if they wanted to.

"Good."

"I have to use the restroom." I walked briskly to the back of the plane and closed the door. The coin looked like an American silver dollar, but it seemed thicker and softer in the middle. It had an odd seam around the circumference. When I tapped the coin on the edge of the sink, it cracked open. As I peeled it into two halves, a curled up scrap of paper fell into the sink, and I caught it just before it went down the drain.

My hands shook as I unrolled it. The paper contained a series of numbers and dots and the word "cabezon." I didn't recognize any pattern or code. What did it mean? Then I noticed the number sequence started with a colon and two forward slashes. Could it be a website address to contact him? What could he want with me? Why wasn't Vander the one to reach out?

It didn't matter. I could never see him or Vander again. The Agency owned me. I was an indentured servant until they were done with me.

This was goodbye forever. I threw the piece of paper in the trash.

This episode of my life was over and a new one was about to begin. I didn't know what it looked like, but I'd wanted it for a long time. I'd never had the courage to do it, but somehow I would find a way to be free of the Agency. It could take years and I might be a damaged shell of myself by then, but I would find a way.

Chapter 20 Stud Services

Vander

The moment we touched down in San Diego after leaving Colombia I started looking for her. Four months later and I still had nothing. Misha was truly gone from my life, and I needed to move on and focus on my work. Too many employees depended on me. I couldn't have my head in the clouds, or I'd make a critical mistake like I did with Teague.

Case in point. On my desk was a multi-million dollar government contract, this one a high-profile assassination in Syria. An incoming call from my brother, Keegan aka Maverick, in Atlanta distracted me from the details.

"What's up, Mav?" I always laughed when I called my own brothers by their nicknames. They did the same to me.

"There's a fuck-ton of Mishas in Moscow." The man had more contacts around the globe than anyone I could think of. I was hoping he'd find a lead on her.

"Yup."

"Needle in an invisible haystack, brother." He sounded discouraged, which was unlike him. "I have minimal access to Russian data. Since all we have is a picture, we need to crack their face recognition database to find her. My best hacker is stumped. Sent it to Rogan as he has some contacts in Veranistaad, but seriously, without a last name, fingerprints, or DNA, we'll never find her."

I grunted. I knew this. I should've gotten her fingerprint or a hair sample, but it all happened so fast, and I really didn't think I'd be in contact with her again.

"Auggie is also turning up nil looking for the entity controlling her."

"You gonna share the reasons behind this?" To protect her, I hadn't told Keegan or anyone at JSOC what happened with Misha. Teague and the team agreed to keep the details vague. We had Teague back and the feds seemed to have forgotten about Skyler Perez for now. Keegan was used to the code of secrecy surrounding the work we did, but he was also risking exposure by attempting to hack into Russian databases.

"No, man. Just curious." And horny and hungry for her.

"What would you do if you found her?"

Fuck her in my bed, on my balcony, on the kitchen table. "Not exactly sure."

"She get under your skin?"

Yes. "No one gets under my skin. She was injured when we sent her back to a sketchy situation. I just wanted to make sure she was okay."

"I'm getting a lot more than curious vibes from you." Keegan was intuitive. Smart and careful. "Word gets out you're socializing with a Russian woman with Colombian ties, could raise red flags."

"I'm not socializing with her. Even if I were, it doesn't mean they can't trust me. If the feds have doubts, they can find someone else to fill their stupid shortfalls. I didn't like the way they stuck their nose into this one before everything went down. They wanted to send in a female assassin to take her out if she learned too much."

"Well shit." We both hated it when the government tried to micromanage the black ops. The foundation and success of our company was based on the fact we acted independently without protocol and red tape to hold us back. "They need us too badly. They won't cross you."

"There's plenty of domestic contracts for us. We don't need them anymore." I was sick of dealing with big brother coming in with their warped ideas of how things should be done.

"We stay on their good side, we can do more business here. We cross the government, they can shut us down and we're shit outta luck."

"I dare them to try and shut us down."

"We're too in bed with them. We keep the contracts." Keegan was the level-headed among us. He could see the big picture when my ego got in the way like it was doing right now.

"You see this new one in Syria?" I asked him.

"Yeah. Fucking insane. Two million for one target?"

"I'm tempted to take it," I admitted.

"Me too." He laughed.

"Then we're fucking insane too."

"Certifiable. Speaking of which, how's Teague?"

I chuckled at his reference to Teague as crazy. "Erratic as hell. Blows off the shrinks. Asks for high-risk assignments. The usual."

"You did all that to save his ass, now he's going out on suicide missions?" Keegan sounded angry, but I wasn't. I knew what Teague was doing. Processing in his own way.

"Let's not tell him about Syria till he gets his head on straight." I may sympathize with my brother's actions right now, but I wouldn't be the one to send him into harm's way again.

"Deal. Check in later, Vander. You and Teague start planning a trip out here for Christmas."

"We're there."

"You taking any clients at Stud Services?"

Stud Services was a little side venture I'd started years ago on a whim. One of Magnum's girls had offered to pay to go out with me. I agreed as a joke, but I was surprised to find that it suited my needs. By adding money to the equation, the women knew it was a transactional relationship. Word spread and I ended up setting up a secret website for it.

"No." Usually I would take up an offer or two to blow off some sexual tension and have some fun, but not this time. This break between missions was all about bonding with Teague and finding her.

He paused. Keegan had one of the sharpest minds in the business. He was about to hit me with something.

"She's your type."

"Misha?"

"Seen you leave with a Russian woman more than once at Siege."

When I was younger, I occasionally met women at Siege, a nightclub in Boston owned by our associate Dallas Monroe. I took those women to hotels to fuck. It had been a long time since I'd done that. It wasn't my scene at all. "Coincidence."

"Then there was that hot Brazillian woman. What was her name?"

"Serafina, but..." I actually couldn't argue with him. I did find South American women attractive, but they weren't my "type."

"Misha good with a weapon?" he asked.

"Better than decent."

"She's all your types combined into one."

I chuckled but didn't disagree with him. He was right. She tripped all my switches. "Never gonna happen. She's gone."

"Right. If she shows up, don't blow it."

"She won't."

"All right. Take care, man."

We ended the call and I leaned back in my chair. I looked out over downtown San Diego and the stark line where the lights ended at the harbor.

Keegan asked all the right questions. Why was I looking for her, and what would I do if I found her? My dick was thinking about tying her to my bed and leaving her there so I could take bites of her whenever I wanted. Show her who's in control after the little power trip she pulled in Cartagena.

The protective side of me was wondering about her contact at the airport and why she couldn't have a dog in Russia.

I knew the answer, but didn't want to accept it. She was probably a Russian asset. Teague and my team were usually right on these things. Even if I found her, I couldn't act on it. She'd be back on the feds' radar and back in danger.

And yet, I couldn't stop thinking about her. Her nightmares about the blue puppy, her sweet core pulsing on my dick, her cries of agony as I listened to the torture through the bug, the burns on her back that felt like scars on my heart, the deep despair in her eyes when she said goodbye to Blue, and the plea in that kiss at the airport. Her lips said *find me, save me, I want you.*

My nature is to answer that call. I don't walk away from a woman begging for help. And yet I had to. If she was truly a Russian agent, everything we'd shared could've been fake and she'd conned me better than anyone ever had. This was all fucked beyond repair.

I stared down at the people on the street going about their business. Eating dinner, drinking in clubs, blissfully unaware of the shit we dealt with on a daily basis.

What if I left the contractor biz behind and became one of those men who hung out in nightclubs? I had to laugh. That would be boring as hell. I needed action like I needed to breathe. I didn't know another way to live.

At that exact moment, an email came through on my Stud Services account. It wasn't unusual to get requests from women, but the sender address caught my attention.

Celeste Perrita.

Light blue puppy in Spanish.

Password: cabezon

I leaned in deep to the screen and blinked several times. How could it be? How had she found my hidden website and successfully sent me a message with the correct password?

This had to be a trick. Someone was pranking me. I clicked on the message and read it eagerly.

Vander, this is Celeste Perrita. I am in town for a brief visit and was hoping to engage your services. However, I have checked your calendar, and it appears you do not have any available time slots. Please respond and let me know if you can fit me in on such short notice. I hope you and Blue are doing well.

I had already hit reply before I finished reading.

Hello, Celeste. Good to hear from you. As luck would have it, I can squeeze you in tonight. Send me your address and get ready because your stud is coming.

I hit send and darted up from my chair. In a few minutes, I was wearing a slate gray Armani suit and tucking my locked and loaded S&W into my hip holster. I swiped my wallet, phone, keys, and shades before checking for her reply.

She had written me back swiftly.

Hotel Coronado. Room 302.

On my way.

Blue, who had been asleep in his bed, popped his head up when he saw me grab my keys. "Let's go, Blue. You have a date."

He dashed to me and jumped so frantically, I had to struggle to get the leash on. "Calm down, you nut."

I wasn't sure who was more excited, me or him.

Chapter 21 Our Little Secret

Misha

The spike of my heels created a polka-dot pattern in the hotel room carpet as I paced the room and fiddled with my hair. This must be how a school girl felt waiting for her handsome prom date to arrive.

I'd seduced sheiks and princes, but an American commando had me shaking in my boots like an anxious virgin.

Why? Because I didn't have the upper hand. I always went into a mission knowing the motivation of the man I was attempting to seduce which made it so much easier to make him give me what I needed, usually information.

With Vander, I didn't know why he agreed to see me, I had no clear purpose except that I wanted to spend time with him, and I had very little chance of controlling his behavior.

It could go wrong in so many ways. If he thought I was here to extract information, he could hurt me, kill me, or arrest me.

But what if it went well? What would that look like?

A night of clandestine sex with the hottest man I'd ever met.

Normal women had nights like this. Why couldn't I do it?

The knock at the door sent a chill through my spine and stole my breath. I smoothed my skirt and walked to the peephole.

Dear Lord, dark reflective shades stared back at me, wavy hair slicked back, a strong chin shaved clean but still shadowed gray. Nothing like the long-haired rugged man I'd met in Colombia.

Could I possibly have contacted some random man through the website Steel gave me? No. This was Vander. He just looked very different.

I opened the door, and we both stood frozen in place staring at each other like strangers. He took off his shades and scanned me from head to toe, most likely also noting that I'd changed significantly from the last time he'd seen me.

My hair was black now, my eyebrows much thicker and darker, my lips painted a deep maroon. He'd only seen me tossed and disheveled as I suffered through an ordeal with no clothes or makeup of my own.

Tonight I wore a reddish-brown fitted leather skirt with bronze accent buttons above the slit in the back. A tight rayon blouse in the same color as the skirt with matching buttons down the front. With heels, I stood three inches taller than the five-foot-eleven he'd seen me at before.

He was easily six-foot-seven so still taller than me, and he looked incredible in a slate gray suit with a white dress shirt, the top button open. No chest hair showing, which had me curious about what was under there.

"Celeste." His deep voice growled out the alias I was using, and I could swear I felt it in my panties.

I gulped down a huge breath of air. Now I knew why I'd flown here and risked everything to see this man again. He commanded every room he entered.

"Vander." I tipped my chin and moved aside, motioning for him to come in as I tried to calm my pittering heart.

He walked in slowly and cautiously, checking all the corners and peering into the bathroom briefly. Convinced the room was clear, he turned to me with cold, dark eyes. "Let's go."

"Go? I thought we could stay here."

"Grab a jacket and your purse. We're going on a date." He sounded angry already. This was not going well at all.

"Oh, I was being facetious. We don't really have to go anywhere. I thought we could just visit?"

"Grab your purse and let's go." The authority in his voice made it very difficult to challenge, but I hadn't planned to leave the room.

"I'd really like to stay incognito." I was indirectly telling him so much. If I were here freely, I wouldn't need to be incognito.

He didn't seem surprised as he slid on his shades. "Slip on a disguise and let's go."

So he knew I was the kind of woman who would wear a disguise, and he was encouraging me to do it now? If he thought I was a spy, he didn't seem put off by it. He seemed like he was willing to play along with my game. I had to make sure he understood the risks. "I don't know who may be following my movements."

He appeared unconcerned. "We'll be discrete. No one will recognize us."

This was crazy. Did he not understand the implications of being seen around town with a Russian agent? Of course he did. He was a smart man and experienced in covert operations. "Oh, um. Let's sit and have a drink first." I motioned to the small refrigerator in the room.

He gripped my upper arm and held it tight. The warmth of his hand seeped into my skin like lava. "Celeste, Blue is in the car waiting for you."

Oh, this man did not play fair. "You are evil."

"So you've told me. Shall we?" He didn't release my arm as he swayed one hand out, motioning for me to precede him to the door, but really he was forcing me out.

"Give me a moment."

He nodded and let me go. In my suitcase, I found a silk scarf and wrapped it around my neck. Since my secret was out, I tied my hair up and slipped on a blonde wig. I glanced at him as I was tucking my roots under the cap. Again, he appeared non-plussed by the fact I traveled with disguises in my suitcase.

I finished and picked up a petite handbag. His eyes went to it. He probably knew I had a weapon in there. Once again, he shocked me by nodding and indicating he was okay with me taking it. With any other man, a disguise and a gun in my bag would raise huge red flags. With Vander, it was standard operating procedure.

I liked sharing this unspoken secret with him.

As he watched me move to the door, he said, "Gorgeous with any color hair."

"What?"

"Auburn, black, blonde. All stunning on you."

Oh my. I rarely blushed, but that compliment from him, after I had basically revealed myself as a spy, meant the world to me. My cheeks heated and I looked down. "Thank you."

And with that, we left my room and embarked on our very not-normal date. My stomach bounded in queasy gymnastics as we stood side-by-side in the elevator. I would see Blue soon, and this would all be worth every second, every risk.

Blue nearly self combusted as we approached. He scratched at the front window of a gunmetal gray muscle car.

Vander opened the door and Blue slipped, twisted, and scratched till he flopped on his belly on the sidewalk. His paws scratched the pavement frantically until he was up again and barreling toward me. I leaned down to catch him as he jumped into my arms. He knocked my chin and almost knocked me over. I laughed and let him lick me. I loved Blue's raw enthusiasm. I couldn't even try to stop him.

"My gosh. Look what a big boy you've become." I tried to hold him still long enough to see the changes in his face. His hair and whiskers reminded me of an adolescent husky mix. Blue was no longer a puppy and I'd missed all the changes. It happens so fast and I missed it. I rubbed his ears and laughed through the chaos.

Vander tugged at his collar and forced him off me. "Blue, you're making me jealous here." He offered me a hand and helped me up. I was still laughing as he guided me into the front seat. Blue jumped up on my lap, tail swiping the open door. He was at least thirty pounds now, but I loved that he still had his goofy puppy energy.

"No. You get in the back." Vander reached for his collar, but I shielded him with my arms.

"Please let me hold him. I only have so much time."

He shook his head and handed me the leash. "Don't let him get over the dash."

"You have limits, puppy. Don't cross the line. Understand? Or the evil guy will pull your teeth out with pliers," I said in a mock commander voice.

Vander chuckled as he closed the door. He was grinning as he walked around the front of the car and folded into the driver's seat. "Take off your wig."

"You don't like the blonde?"

"I like her fine, but I like the real you more."

I felt an embarrassing blush blooming in my cheeks as I removed the pins and tugged the wig cap from my scalp. I ran my finger through my real hair to make sure I got all the pins.

He smiled as he watched me. "Turn your cell phone off," he ordered.

Blue panted with his long pink tongue hanging out. He leaped for the center console, but I held him back with a firm grip. "I already did. Whatdaya think I'm a rookie?" I gave him just enough leash to leap forward and lick Vander's face.

Vander stared at me unmoving. "No. I might not know what you are, but rookie is not on the list of possibilities."

"Oh." My cheeks felt hot, and my tummy flip-flopped. God, why did he have to be everything I'd ever dreamed of but could never have?

Chapter 22 Honor

I enjoyed driving around San Diego with Vander. The city was beautiful and bright. The car handled smoothly and smelled good filled with his clean scent. My worries about the Agency and Colombia seemed so far away in this sunny utopia.

After a short drive along the coast, we pulled into the harbor and stopped in a parking lot at the end where it was less crowded.

When Vander climbed out and came around to open my door, Blue went crazy again, tail swishing around in the car like a flag. He hopped down and performed an epic shake from snout to tail.

With one hand on the small of my back, the other holding Blue's leash, he guided us out on a wooden dock to a spot where a huge yacht was moored. The darkness concealed the extent of it, but it felt like standing next to a towering cruise ship. He casually hopped over the gap and stepped up onto the yacht with Blue, who made the jump like an old pro. Blue turned back to me and wagged his tail, sniffing down at the water, like *hey, jump over, it's fin*e. His eyes went a little wild too, like *you are coming with us, righ*t? Oh, I felt terrible for abandoning my pup, but he was better off with Vander.

He lowered a set of steps to the dock and offered me a hand. "Welcome aboard Honor." He helped me up the stairs using his injured arm, so I could assume the wound I had inflicted on him had healed.

"Is this your boat?" The deck swayed slightly beneath me. The buoyancy made my stomach queasy for a second. Blue

135

licked my knees, and Vander released his leash with a snap which sent Blue bounding down the deck to the stern of the boat.

"Technically, it's the company's yacht, but yeah, it's mine when I need it."

He flipped on an exterior light and opened the cabin with a key. He flipped on lights that illuminated luxurious white and navy blue furniture. As each light came on, I felt a jolt of electricity. Vander's cool calmness as he traversed the deck of a yacht while wearing a manicured suit had me breathless. I came here to have a one-night stand with him. I didn't expect all of this.

Blue had made a complete round and returned to us like, *see my cool boat*? I patted his head and bent down to give him a hug. He was the best dog ever.

"Come. Let me show you." Vander held out a strong masculine hand that felt warm and rough as I slipped my fingers into it. We walked to the bow and peered out over the lights reflecting off the bay.

"It's beautiful here."

"Not the worst place to be based."

"I assume because this boat is in the harbor near the naval training center, that you are a sailor, perhaps a SEAL?"

"You didn't hear me say it." He looked out over the water without making eye contact with me. "But yes, retired. I'm trusting you with that information especially since it's pretty much obvious by now."

"I'm not surprised. You're a highly skilled fighter. I figured your team was special ops."

He nodded but still didn't look at me. He clearly couldn't tell me any more than that.

"How often do you come here?"

"On the occasions where she's docked here and I'm in town, I take her and Blue out when I'm not busy. It's rare though."

"And when you say busy, you mean the escort service?"

He laughed. "No. I didn't mean that."

"What keeps you busy? I'm curious."

He looked down at me like he was debating how much to tell me. "I run a private military contractor operation."

This also was not a surprise. He was obviously the leader of the team I met. "So you're not a full-time escort?"

He threw his head back and belly-laughed. "You keep coming back to that so let me lay it out. I'm not really an escort. It's something that evolved as a way to... meet a need."

"Sex?"

"Yes." He looked away again. "And companionship. Basically, a friend of one of Magnum's girlfriends..."

"How many girlfriends does he have?"

He sputtered and started talking faster. "Let's just say an acquaintance of Magnum's offered to pay a large sum of money to go on a date with me. I reluctantly agreed because she was a nice woman and Magnum was pressuring me. It went better than I thought it would. It was sort of a blind date with a solid agreement behind it. It helped establish limits." His voice had lost some of his usual confidence.

"You seem nervous talking about this."

"I rarely speak of it, and it's become less important lately."

"Why?"

"I haven't felt the need like I did before, and it's not meeting it in the way it did when I was younger."

"Ahh." So meaningless sex was losing its appeal for him. Interesting.

"Anyway, word spread, and I had a long list of women wanting to become clients. When I desired the company of a woman, I would pick one and fulfill her wishes. It worked out well for both of us, and it was a nice diversion from the world of special ops."

We walked in silence to an upper deck that was situated with rattan couches around a low table. With a firm grip on my hand, he drew me in close and slipped an arm over my shoulder as we settled into the thick cotton cushions. "What would you like to drink?"

"I'm fine right now. Tell me more about this escort business."

He chuckled and leaned his nose close to my ear. "You are persistent, Kroshka."

There it was. I never thought I'd hear it again. "I assume these women are paying top dollar for your attention."

"Yes..."

"So you are being paid for sex."

"Sex is not included in the agreement. If it happens between consenting adults, that's outside of the deal. There's been a few women I did not sleep with on our dates."

"A few? Why?"

He rubbed his forehead and stared out over the water. "I never talk about this with anyone and here you have me confessing within an hour after I picked you up."

"I find it fascinating, and I know something about exchanging sex for services."

His face darkened. "There's a huge difference. I'm not forced to do anything. I do it because it's mutually enjoyable for the woman and myself. It avoids miscommunication about relationships and expectations. I'm gone all the time. I can't form any attachments, and they know that before we meet."

"Can't or won't?"

"Jesus, woman. Can we change the subject? You spill your guts about your sex life and then I'll tell you more."

"I have no sex life." I smiled sadly. "I told you. I'm a whore."

"No. You're a Russian agent and use sex to seduce your mark. Not the same."

I gasped hearing him say it aloud. I figured that he knew the truth, but it was another thing to hear him say it. At least he didn't use the derogatory word *spy*. "Like you said. The difference is you are not forced. I have no choice. I can't refuse an assignment. It is expected the mark will form an attachment, and I will not."

"And how does that affect you?"

"My life is not my own. I don't have the luxury of choosing a sexual partner. Never has a man inquired about my preferences. It's extremely functional on my part. They, of course, act out all their perversions on me because I am disposable, nothing to them. Unless they become attached, then I have power over them outside the bedroom. But physically, I have no right to request anything that would make the sex enjoyable for me."

"That is absolutely unacceptable."

"It's my life."

"Have you ever been in love?"

"What is love? There was a time once when I did such a convincing job of making a man fall in love with me, I believed I'd fallen in love myself."

"What happened with him?"

Oh no. I didn't expect to talk to him about this. "I am watched very closely."

"What happened with him?" He repeated his question.

He had been open with me so far, so I should return the favor. "His name was Alvaro. He was lower level in Ruben Duran's cartel operation. They overheard me talking about him with a female friend. I was struggling with my feelings, not sure if I was falling in love or just getting sucked in by the situation. I confided in a woman I had befriended."

"And then?"

The haunting guilt filled my chest. "He died unexpectedly."

"They killed him?"

I nodded slightly. "I'm not sure, but it appeared I indirectly caused his death." I'd only just considered falling in love with him, and he lost his life.

"My God, Misha." He stood and walked away from me. He ran his hands through his hair and looked out over the bay for a long time. Blue paced between us like he was trying to connect us again.

When he didn't return, I said to his back, "Please don't worry about me."

He spun on me, heat burning in his face. "Why did you come here?"

I flinched back, surprised by his sudden change in mood.

"Why did you come here, honestly? Don't give me some bullshit answer either. We're beyond that."

I didn't realize we were beyond anything, but I decided to be honest with him. "I came to see you."

"Why? Are you here on a recon mission?"

"No."

"What did they do to you when you returned?"

"Nothing. They believed my story. They ran me through some training. I decided to fly here on a whim. I expected to stay one night, see you and Blue, and return to Moscow to receive my next assignment. I'm not here as an agent. I'm here as me. Whoever I am. Misha." My hands flapped uselessly at my sides. This body was all that I had that was me.

"Why did you want to see me?" he asked.

"You're putting me on the spot."

"Yes. Because you've brought this problem to my door and confirmed again what I suspected, that you're forced to sleep with men and your entire life is not your own because you answer to tyrants who control your every move to the point they would murder someone you cared about to keep you from leaving them."

I lowered my head. It hurt to hear him say it with such venom.

"Why did you come to me? Tell me now." He was growing frustrated with my evasion.

"I came to you because I wanted you to make love to me." My voice wavered. "I told myself I came for sex, but now that I see you, and we've talked, and you want honesty. I came here to ask you to make love to me. Not Skyler or Celeste. Misha. Not a Russian spy or whore. Just a woman who doesn't know who she is and has never been truly loved by a man in that way."

He stepped closer and pointed at me. "With me, you got a taste of who you are and what it could be like and you want more of that, but I know how this will end." His fists clenched as he paced away. "If I give you what you need, I mean really give it to you like only I can, it'll wreck you. You'll return to Moscow, they'll force you to sleep with another disgusting man, and you'll break. Whatever strength you think you'll draw from will evaporate. No one can tolerate that. Not even once much less a lifetime." The scar on his face curled inward with his frown, and he truly looked like a viper preparing to strike.

I shouldn't have come. It was foolish of me to assume he'd accept me as I am, flaws and all. "Perhaps we should try this again some other time."

"When? When you're forty? Or fifty?" His volume blared and I flinched back. "How much of your life do you want to live having never been treated with decency and respect?"

Chapter 23 Three Packages

Blue's urgent barking caused us both to pause and look. Down on the dock, two shadowy figures approached the yacht. I ducked into the stairwell and tugged on his hand. "Someone's here."

He didn't take cover but kept his gaze on the dock. "Yeah, I know. Those are my men."

I climbed up out of the stairwell as two men carrying large insulated boxes in their hands boarded the ship. Both of them looked familiar, but their names didn't come to me instantly. They were clean shaven, wearing jeans and T-shirts, relaxed grins on their faces as they greeted Blue.

Vander shook out his neck and cleared his throat to break the tension between us. Our conversation had escalated quickly, and the carefree attitude of his friends reminded me we were on a pleasure yacht in a beautiful harbor and so far had remained undetected.

"Yo, Stud. Brought your date some chow." That must be Magnum. I'd heard him call Vander Stud before. He was teasing Vander for his Stud Escort Service. I had to laugh too now that I knew the context.

The other man didn't say anything but as soon as he came into the light, I recognized him as Axel without a beard. Vander and I walked over to greet them. "You remember Magnum and Axel. This is Skyler aka Misha."

"Hello."

"How's your back?" Axel asked me.

"Healed. Thank you."

"Good. We brought food and we'll pilot the ship." Magnum handed the large insulated package to Vander.

"That's nice of you."

Agitation rolled off Vander. He hovered over me like he was ready to burst into motion.

"We're also providing security. You'll be safe," Axel said.

"I trust I will."

They seemed to like that because they grinned and stared at me.

"Get to work, then. Cast her off." Vander smacked Magnum hard on the shoulder and tossed the keys to Axel. Both men turned and started working the ropes on the boat, chuckling as they followed orders. Blue danced along happily with them.

"You. Come with me." Vander carried the food down to the cabin below and I followed him. He set the carrying case on a seat bench and began unpacking it. First, he placed a bottle of wine and a corkscrew in the center of the table. He moved quickly, setting circular plate containers side by side. His shoulders were still tight and his jaw clenched as he placed two wine glasses and silverware next to the plates. I watched him quietly as he jammed the corkscrew into the cork and pulled it out with so much force it made a loud pop. He unscrewed the cork and tossed it over to the sink.

"Let's eat. Have a glass of wine. Relax."

"You're still angry. We don't have to..."

"I'm not angry."

"You just opened that bottle of wine like it was a hand grenade."

He looked from the open bottle in his hand to the sink where he'd thrown the cork as if he didn't remember doing it.

"I can hardly relax now." The engine beneath us sputtered and hummed and the boat moved slowly forward. "You've called in reinforcements and we're heading out to sea. Are you taking me captive again?"

He slammed the bottle down on the table and his eyes narrowed. "You contacted me. You asked for discretion. I provided that, at very short notice I might add. The men are here for your security. You may leave at any time. Say the word, we'll turn this ship around and drop you off on the dock."

"If that's what you want. Fine. Tell Magnum and Axel to return to port. You're clearly not the man I thought you were. I risked my life to come here to see you today. I've made myself vulnerable by telling you the truth, and you've rejected me every step of the way." I walked past him to the door.

"I'm not rejecting you."

I paused on the first step of the stairs.

"It's quite the opposite. It infuriates me to see a woman being treated like you are. Suffering needlessly and yet returning time and again for more abuse. You're asking me to make love to you knowing full well you'll go back to him."

I didn't know which *him* he was referring to. He didn't know about Sergei. Maybe he meant Duran or my brother. There were many men who controlled my actions. "I can't leave," I said quietly. He was asking the impossible.

"But you want to."

"It's not an option."

"Everything is optional."

With that I was done being vulnerable in front of him. He was twisting this all around and turning it on me, making it about leaving the Agency. That wasn't why I came here at all. I hated his arrogant assumption he knew anything about me. "Why are you doing this? I didn't contact you to have you stand in judgment of my life. I wanted to fuck," I spat it in his face, "in a hotel room and leave." I made an X with my hands and chopped away the invisible strings tying me to this man and the tormenting words he was shoving in my face. "That's it. You run a fucking escort service. You don't get this concept?"

He stalked toward me slowly, his eyes darkening to black orbs. I'd pressed the robot's remote control button that set him into ambush mode. "Right. We have three packages, Miss Perrito. Neat." He forced my back up against the wall and pressed his massive body against mine. "On the rocks." He took my hands and locked them over my head as he thrust his hips into my belly. I panted into his mouth that was just a breath away. "Or shaken and stirred with a twist of danger."

He hooked his knee around my leg and flipped me off the wall. I grunted as his torso pushed my head down, bending me at the waist, his foot spreading my legs. I wobbled in my heels and braced my wrists on the stairs. He jammed his groin into the crack of my ass. One of his strong hands pinned my wrists to the step while the other wrapped around my neck and applied pressure. Not enough to constrict my breathing, but enough to send the message he wouldn't hesitate to do it. "What can I get you, ma'am?"

Chapter 24 Hungry

I struggled against his hold, but he had me locked in a steel cage. I couldn't think straight. I should be afraid, but I was instantly wet between my legs, my body heated and sweating, my breath ragged and raspy. I wanted the shaken-and-stirred-with-twist-of-danger package. Absolutely. I rarely allowed myself the guilty pleasure of being reckless and wild. Always calculated and cautious. Only with Vander could I take a risk like this.

"You want to be kidnapped again. Don't you? Be my captive. You loved the edge of danger in Colombia. Knowing you couldn't trust me. I couldn't trust you. We were both waiting to see who would take advantage and kill the other. Is that what you like?"

"No." Yes.

"Bullshit. I'd bet you couldn't even get off without the threat of death."

"Fuck you." I could get off without threats, but otherwise, he'd hit the nail on the head. I loved the insecurity of exposure, especially with him because deep down I wanted to trust him, even though I knew it was wrong in every sense.

He wrapped a solid arm around my waist and hoisted me off my feet like I weighed nothing. My shoes fell to the floor and he stepped over them. He dropped me on my stomach on the bed at the back of the cabin. "I'm going to tie you to this bed and take from you at my leisure. We can sail this ship to China, and I'll have days to draw from you. Tease you. Take what I need and force you to accept the truth."

Oh yes. I wanted that too. I didn't even know exactly what the truth was, but I wanted him to make me face it in a way that only he could do. "I have to be back. They expect me."

He lay down flat on top of me, his heat and weight devouring me and pressing me to the bed. The textures of our clothes meshed together in a crinkly rub of smooth and crisp. "Who?"

I didn't answer.

"*They* are going to be disappointed. You're not gonna make your rendezvous. You got captured on your little side trip, and now you have to pay the price."

Lordy lord, I had no idea if he was being serious or not, but I was betting he was bluffing. If I asked him to, he'd stop and turn this boat around like he offered just minutes ago before this all went from civilized yet tense to savage attack. I had zero desire to ask him to stop. I wanted to see how far he would take this maneuver and how much I could handle.

First, a little test. I elbowed him in the gut hard and heard his grunt. My feet were free so I plunged my ankles into his lower back. I barely made a dent in his rock hard body. Bucking my hips did little to dislodge him.

It merely incited him to pin my hands over my head. "You wanna fight, Kroshka?"

There it was. *Little one.* Yes, he enjoyed this as much as me. "Always." Making myself smaller and sinking into the bed, I was able to loosen the pressure of his weight and twist my hips until I was facing him. He was forced to let my wrists spin in his grip or he'd break my bones. I snapped up at him, trying to bite his earlobe that was close to my teeth, but he reacted quickly, flinching back just enough to avoid it. My teeth slapped shut with a loud clap.

He held both my wrists in one hand and reached over my head to grab something out of the storage in the headboard. I bit his side through his dress shirt and rammed my knee into his balls.

He growled. "Watch it. I bite back."

I hoped so. Our wrestling match made it very clear he was much bigger and stronger than me. Even my hardest jabs barely phased him. I lost some of my fight as my muscles strained.

He unearthed metal handcuffs from the container above my head and deftly smacked them over my wrist. He pulled my arm and hooked the cuff around a decorative spindle at the head of the bed. It connected to the storage box, so I couldn't slide over the top.

My lips trembled and my brain was utterly scrambled. If he wasn't playing, I was in deep trouble. My heart pounded like it would burst through my ribcage.

He grunted and climbed higher up my body, knees holding my shoulders down as he restrained my other hand to the opposite side. I jammed my knee into his back as hard as I could. He lowered his head and grinned. "You're a good fighter. I like that."

Okay. That sexy smile was not something a man who was truly kidnapping me would do. This was play, but it was still terrifying because it was unknown, unplanned, volatile.

The edge of the metal cuffs dug into my wrists as he slid down to my feet. Oh boy. He had more cuffs attached to his hip. When he went for one leg, I jammed my toes into his neck. He quickly and calmly subdued my free foot while he attached a pair of cuffs to the bottom of the bed. The metal bit into my ankle, and I had to stop struggling or I'd tear my skin.

When he yanked my other leg out, my skirt pulled tight, and he couldn't reach the fourth spindle. He assessed the situation, pulled again, and saw that my skirt wasn't going to give. He tried to slip it up my hips but it was too tight. With a grunt, he drew a knife from the back pocket of his slacks and hooked the bottom of my skirt.

Holy cow. Another tremor of terror flashed through me. I was completely at his mercy. And yet, I loved it. He was right. The edge of danger turned me on.

He smiled as he sliced the fabric from my thigh to my navel, revealing my black lace panties. His eyes riveted between my legs like he was transfixed.

I still had one leg free, and now I was unrestrained by my skirt, so I speared my foot deep and hit his groin. It had to hurt his straining dick. He moaned like I hadn't hit him and bent down to suck on my mound through the fabric like he was drawn to it by a magnetic field. He held my loose foot with one hand and dove in with his hot wet tongue.

Oh my. It felt like sharp shards of glass were ripping through every inch of my skin. My legs trembled as I bucked up into his face. Do not stop, Vander. Whatever you do, do not stop now.

He inhaled loudly and sucked my mound till the fabric soaked through, making every swipe of his tongue and his teeth more overwhelming.

I cried when he suddenly stopped. "No!"

He chuckled and skimmed up my body as I struggled to inhale a solid breath. He plunged his tongue into my mouth and took it. No preamble, no invitation.

I didn't want to resist anymore. I wanted this kiss to go on forever. I wrapped my free leg around his strong hips and tugged him closer. He groaned and smashed his hard cock into my core. My hips jerked up, answering him back. Our breaths came fast and heavy, both of us exerted from the tussle.

I jammed the heel of my foot between his ass cheeks and rubbed. It was like being wedged between two rocks.

"You, my captive, have mesmerized me with your sweet pussy and taken advantage with your free foot. Unscrupulous."

I laughed. "I'll use any leverage I can."

He smirked and slid down my body again, kissing my chest, navel, and between my legs along the way. His lips left a trail of sparks in their wake.

Even with my skirt cut open the last pair of cuffs didn't give him enough slack to reach the last spindle. He removed the cuffs and sat on his knees on the bed, looking at the conundrum.

"Leave my foot free."

"No. You cannot be trusted with an inch of freedom."

He loosened his belt and slipped it from his slacks.

"Oh no." I yanked my foot back, but he gripped it tighter as he threaded it through the buckle and around my ankle. He pulled it tight and fashioned a knot around the spindle. "The harder you pull, the tighter it will get."

I gasped in fake exasperation.

He backed away to examine his work and brushed his hands like he was shaking off dust. He removed his jacket and dropped it on a bench. "I'm hungry after that workout. I think I'll get some food."

No! "You are evil."

"Yes and you love it."

I laughed. "I do not. You flatter yourself."

His ass looked fantastic in his suit as he walked over to the table and picked up a plate of food from the insulated container. He lifted the lid and steam rose up by his face. "This looks delicious. Almost as good as eating you."

"Ha."

He sauntered back over to the bed and it dipped as he sat by my hip. "We have some juicy steak strips, medium rare, fluffy whipped potatoes, and roasted vegetables with lots of garlic and butter."

He tilted his head back, opened his mouth, and dropped in a chunk of steak. He grinned as he chewed it with his mouth closed. "Mmm. Want some?" He dangled a piece of steak in the air, a bit of juice dripping down onto his plate.

I was still turned on and high from his mouth on me, but I managed to say, "No. You'll probably poison me."

"I wouldn't poison you. C'mon. Open up. Let me feed you."

"No."

"All right. More for me." He tossed the piece of steak in his mouth. He swirled some potatoes on a fork and held it up to my mouth. It smelled divine so I parted my lips and he fed me. It tasted better than it smelled.

He also fed me some vegetables, and I started to relax. Now I was sure he was playing with me, and I loved the contrast with his gravely serious side.

He poured wine into my mouth and kissed the drops that ran down my chin.

"What do we have for dessert? Looks like a little cheesecake." He chuckled and brought it over to me with a spoon.

He scooped up a bite and offered it to me. I swirled it with my tongue to tease him.

His eyes watched my tongue and his mouth dropped open a little. "Oh, now you are evil. You'll pay for that."

Chapter 25 Captive

He slipped the bite of cheesecake into his mouth and bent forward to kiss me. We shared a mushy, sticky, sweet kiss, our tongues battling to taste the dessert plus each other. Kissing Vander was an intimate, sexy treat. It broke down the wall he constructed between us with his tough guy act.

He finished kissing me and looked into my eyes. "Yum."

"Are you going to let me go now?"

He laughed. "I have only just begun to torture you." He climbed over me and straddled my hips. "Look at you. Tied up and helpless. You can't fight me or take control. I think I'll take my time." He pressed soft open mouthed kisses down the column of my throat. He worked open the buttons of my blouse and sliced the strap of my bra, releasing my breasts from their constraints. "Absolutely beautiful."

I had nice breasts. I knew that. They were my greatest assets. When a man leered at them, I thought I had power over him, but with Vander, he had all the power. I was at his mercy.

He pulled one nipple into his mouth and bit down, causing a full-body shiver. Everywhere he touched me turned me into a live wire. His hand moved between my legs, and my belly fluttered. Was this it? Was he finally going to let me come?

He massaged my clit in unhurried circles that drove me absolutely wild. I arched my back and bent my knees as much as the restraints would allow. I was climbing again and Vander was bringing me there.

He stopped again. I growled. He sliced my panties at each hip and the fabric fell away, leaving me exposed while he was still fully clothed.

"Please," I moaned.

He worked two thick fingers deep inside. "God, you're so wet for me."

They curled up and teased a sensitive spot that felt so good I had to squeeze my eyes shut as it passed through me. This long slow torture was driving me absolutely mad. I thrashed my head from side to side.

His hot mouth came up to hover over my lips. "I like watching you like this. I can touch you however I like, tease you as long as I want, and you can't stop me. But you don't want me to stop. Do you?"

"No." Don't you dare stop.

"You want me to keep going and make you come?"

"Yes." Faster please. Much, much faster.

"Over and over?" He twirled the pad of his thumb in a lazy circle in time with his taunting words.

"Yes."

"Then you want me to fuck you good and hard so you forget your name? All of them? You'll forget everything except for my hard cock ramming into you, bringing you higher and making you see stars. Because you need this. You need someone to give you what you want. You need someone to care about your orgasm, your pleasure, because no one ever has. Correct?"

Now? Vander was picking now to start talking? Lord help me. This would never end.

"Yes. No one ever has. Not like this." I answered quickly, not daring to say anything that might get him talking again.

"Good. I want to give you what no one has given you before." He sunk his teeth into my shoulder above the collar bone, and I gasped. He was still fully clothed and working me like I belonged to him. And right then in that moment, I did belong to him, body and soul.

"Right now you need to come." Yes! I do. "Let it fully happen. Don't fight it. You deserve it. This is all for you. It's not about pleasing me or getting anything from me. This is one-hundred percent pure pleasure for you. Let your body feel it."

"Yes, yes. Hurry." If you would stop talking and get to the business of pleasing me, that would be great.

Finally, he shut up and slipped away. I couldn't see him, but I felt his mouth back between my legs, this time without the fabric blocking us and it was glorious. His tongue flicked and pressed and twirled on my clit as his lips sucked it deeper and released again. Yes! I felt like screaming but I didn't want him to start talking again so I bit my lip, hard, like drawing blood hard.

He didn't need to instruct me. I automatically forgot who I was, I couldn't possibly fight it, and couldn't be bothered about his enjoyment.

My arms and legs being constrained forced all my attention to that one spot where his mouth was pleasing me. His growl vibrated through my core as he sunk two fingers inside me and curled them up. Within seconds, a powerful tidal wave washed over me and stole my breath.

I gasped and moaned as my body convulsed on his fingers over and over, pure euphoria coursing through me. His wicked tongue kept teasing to drag out every last quake. It felt unending. Perpetual. Finally, as it ebbed, he rose up over me to kiss my lips. "Good girl."

"Untie me. I want to touch you." This was so unfair. So one-sided. He had a chiseled body, and he needed to give me access to it.

"Ahh, sneaky. But that will make you wonder if I'm enjoying it. This is all for you."

"If it's for me, I want to see you naked."

His eyes narrowed. "No."

"Please. Let me see you. I've already seen your gorgeous dick. Take off that suit. Strip for me. That's what I want. What I've dreamed of since I met you."

"Since you met me? When you were trying to kill me?"

"Okay. Since you brought me a puppy to be exact."

"So I brought you the puppy and you wanted to see me naked?"

"Yes. Look at you. You're fantastic. Get naked, untie me, and let me touch you."

He tapped his chin with his index finger then licked it. "Mmm. I'm really enjoying having you at my disposal."

"You said it's for me. I need to know that you trust me. Let me touch you freely. Without suspicion. That's what I need more than anything." I hadn't planned to say it, but now that it was out there, it changed the dynamic of this. It wasn't just sex anymore. It was a symbol of breaking barriers. Even if it was only temporary, if he truly saw me for who I was, he'd let me into his fortress right now.

He crawled on top of me and kissed me as one hand reached up and released the cuffs. When the pressure left, overwhelming joy surged through me. Vander was opening a door for me.

He still had me pinned with his body when he removed the other cuff. My arms burned as I brought them down, but I quickly forgot as my hands landed on the insanely solid muscles of his back. I had never in my life been this close to a man this rugged and sinewy, and the fact he trusted me with my hands on him made it all so much more important.

After he released my legs, he stood to unbutton his shirt. His eyes turned black as coal as I slipped my hand between my legs and touched my sensitive bundle of nerves. He pulled a condom from his pocket and held it in his teeth as he opened his slacks, sliding them down his hips in the sexiest striptease I'd ever seen. Black boxer briefs clung to him like a second skin, a huge erection tenting the fabric.

He freed his dick and grasped it as he opened the condom and slipped it over his massive length before climbing back between my legs.

Finally, his hot body came down and fit together with mine like a jigsaw puzzle. I dragged my nails across his back, smooth silk over steel, as he positioned himself. He didn't tense or pull back. He was comfortable with my nails scraping his back. He wasn't worried I'd stab him or break his neck.

My mouth lined up with his bicep and the scar that was healing. I kissed it gently. "I'm sorry I shot you," I whispered.

He dropped his forehead to my neck. "It's okay, babe. Remember, I untied you because you promised not to think about me. You wanted this for you, and *this* is for you." He pushed the tip of his giant cock between my folds and my legs trembled.

Finally, it was time. It felt like it took us forever to get here, but it was worth every second of torture to feel him waiting at the precipice like this, his muscles taut, his focus fully on me. Losing all semblance of patience, I wrapped my legs around him and gave the final push that drove his hips forward. He filled and stretched me so hard and deep I could barely breathe.

He groaned in my ear. "Fuck. So wet. Tight. I can't..."

"Yes. Please, give it to me," I begged. I was so desperate and beyond all sense of pride. He rocked his hips, mashing his groin against my clit. That alone made my stomach clench and an orgasm threatened. I didn't know what was holding him back, but he didn't need to worry. If he wanted to be rough, I'd love it. He could do no wrong at this point. "Don't hold back. It's okay. I trust you."

He needed to hear it as bad as I needed to say it. He reared up and slammed back in, smashing my clit, his balls and hips slapping against my thighs and butt.

He growled and gave it all to me, jamming me over and over, crashing into my clit like thunder and dragging it deliciously before blasting in again. I tilted my hips and pushed back to meet each thrust. He was an incredible fucking machine, wrenching another orgasm from deep in my soul.

The tremor jolted through me and blinded me. Absolute bliss. Each drag and smack drew it out, amplified it, until there was nothing left of me except this orgasm. I was lost to the world. The only thing I could feel was his hot body over me, his rigid cock scorching a trail inside me, and my body's eager response to it all.

My nails dug into his skin, and he kept ramming with ferocious, frightening, unstoppable power.

And then I couldn't answer back with my hips anymore because he'd lifted me off the bed. His big arm wrapped around the top of my ass as he rose to his knees. He was working me like a battering ram, plunging me down on his cock as veins popped in his neck and arms. Trying to move was useless. He had me fully under his control, and I could do nothing but enjoy the harsh slap of our bodies above the bed.

"Give it to me, now, Vander. I want to see it." I'd said it to him before about his cock. This time I meant his climax. I wanted to see how this out-of-control car chase finally ended.

He raised his gaze to mine and his eyes simmered with something so primal and savage, his entire body covered in a sheet of glistening sweat. His mouth drew down, and I could almost see it burning and chewing through him. He crashed us together one last time and held it there. He grunted and exploded, his face flashing red before a huge blast of air rushed from his mouth. Even with the condom, I could feel him pumping his release inside me. I held my breath and took it all in. He was giving me a gift allowing me to see him like this, totally wild and carnal.

I held onto his shoulders as he rode through it, and I quivered through the aftershocks of mine. He held me suspended in air as we heaved in strangled breaths.

After long moments, he collapsed on top of me into a sweaty exhausted heap, kissing my neck and humming. "Fucking loved that."

"I thought it was for me." I chuckled.

"It was for both of us." He kissed my lips as he smiled.

He lay next to me utterly relaxed for a while. That was so much more than I'd hoped for. I'd fantasized that he'd be incredible and we could recreate some of the magic we'd discovered last time.

I had no idea this would turn into my ultimate dream date complete with kinky sex, his violent release, and an obstacle overcome between us.

He'd trusted me at his most vulnerable while he was naked and overcome with his orgasm. I'd wanted one more night with him and he'd given me that in spades.

I also received much more than I'd expected. I'd been changed. After this, it would be impossible to return to my next assignment and board a plane to risk my life for Russia again. I'd rather die. I simply could not do it no matter the consequences. I almost cried from the weight of it as it hit me.

"You're staying the night here with me," Vander mumbled from his restful position next to me.

"I have responsibilities and expectations," I said halfheartedly, knowing he would never feel obligated to return me to anyone.

He rolled half on top of me. "Fuck that. I'm holding you captive, remember?" His arm squeezed my waist.

I'd acquiesce tonight because tomorrow would be a new day. I wasn't sure how it would unfold, but however I severed myself from the SVG, Vander could not be involved. I'd created the mess that was my life and it was my duty to sort it out. If it resulted in my death, at least I'd had this moment with Vander. I'd have to push him away to break free, but I would never give Sergei or the SVG any inroad to sinking their toxic claws into Vander or his family.

Chapter 26 Unavailable

Vander

Neither one of us had nightmares when we were together. I didn't want to read too much into it, but it said something about us.

After breakfast, she'd thanked Magnum and Axel and we'd loaded Blue in the car. I didn't take her back to Hotel Del right away. I wanted one last chance to get through to her.

I took her to a parking lot at the beach and pulled up next to the sand so she could see the waves hitting the shore. Salty air filled the car as I lowered the windows and Blue stuck his head out from the back seat.

"This really is one of the most beautiful corners of the world." Blue climbed between the seats onto her lap, and she laughed as he stuck his head out her window, his tail flying in the space between us.

"Get in the back, Blue."

They both looked at me to see if I meant it.

"In the back." Blue reluctantly stepped over the center the console and made his way back to his seat. He could still stick his head out the window so he was happy.

"I should get to the hotel," she said wistfully.

"I don't like you going back to him."

"It's not one man."

Good. She was finally sharing something. "Tell me then who I have to kill to get to you."

She shook her head. "You can't kill them. They are every-where. Even if you killed Sergei, another comrade would rise up to take his place and I'd answer to him."

Sergei. Now I had a name. "Is Sergei KGB?"

"No. SVG. It's a satellite project of the KGB, but Sergei runs most of it himself. KGB only gets involved if something goes wrong."

"Tell me how you ended up there."

She sighed. "I went into the Agency at age eleven. My fa-ther had told them I was smart and pretty. My breasts devel-oped early. They came and took me to the training center to live."

She was sharing fast and freely now like she'd finally opened the dam and it was flowing full force. "Your father did that to you?"

"It's a long story. I don't even know how to tell you. He's dead now. That's all that matters. He wasn't my biological fa-ther anyway. My mother said my real father was an American diplomat of Colombian descent. She said that's why I looked so different from my father."

As happy as I was that she was opening up, I absolutely hat-ed to hear the extent of what she'd been through.

"I believe my father always hated me because I didn't look like him. I have no proof, but I think he sold me to the Agency to get rid of me. My mother fought for me, I rebelled, they killed my mother and showed me the pictures of her body." She covered her face with her hands. "They said they would kill my brother next. I tried to follow the rules but made a lot of dumb mistakes. Then my father died. My entire family was wiped out in a year. My brother is all I have left."

This was so much worse than I'd imagined. "Say the word and I'll get you out."

She shook her head. "This isn't the kind of thing you get out of. Not alive."

"I didn't make it to where I am in life believing impossible problems didn't have solutions. You just gotta be creative and persistent. I can see you're scared, but I'm not."

"I'm not scared."

"You are or you'd do it. You have so much repressed rage. You're dead inside. There's this moat around you because you can't be who you are. It's killing you and you're trying to destroy yourself to solve it, but that's not the answer."

She looked down. "Please just let me handle it."

"I'm not stopping you from going back to your life. I'm just saying this doesn't have to be it. We can have more. Imagine how it could be if you were mine."

She inhaled and let it out in a ragged breath. "There are so many reasons why we can't. We play on opposite teams. Your career is on the line if you're associated with me. My life is at stake if I don't follow orders. Take away all of that, which is impossible to take away, and neither one of us is emotionally healthy or available."

"And how do you figure all this?"

"Which issue of the magazine would you like? First issue, you are utterly void of compassion."

"I do not lack compassion."

"You wanted to torture me and bought me a puppy instead because someone talked you into it."

"How do you know that?"

"You told me as much, and I know the life you lead. Compassion is a weakness."

"Compassion is not high on my list of priorities for doing my job," I admitted. "Second issue?"

"You think I'm a version of your mom you can save. She sounds like she had a messed up life. You took that on as your own responsibility. I don't know. Maybe you feel guilty about how you solved that one, but whatever the results, it's given you this hero complex."

She was pointing a lot of jabs at me, but ignoring the important part. "You told me you were a whore. Your eyes are lifeless. They have sucked your soul dry."

"There's some truth to that too, but I'm not your mother and I don't need a hero."

I reached my arm behind her seat and leaned over the console to get in her space. "I think you need someone to help you see the light."

She pulled back and fought the intimacy of my closeness. "There is no light at the end of this, and when you get my hopes up it only makes it hurt more when I have to go back."

I sat back in my seat and stared out at the ocean. "You came to see me. You wanted something."

"I wanted sex. You have an incredible cock." She said it without conviction.

"We both know there was a lot more than sex going on last night."

"No. You tell yourself that."

I didn't believe her. I could feel the lie under her words. "Your body told me that. You've ached for a man to anticipate your needs, to push your limits, to make it totally about you.

You're a sexual being. You have desires that demand answers. It's normal to explore that part of yourself, especially after the way you were taught skewed everything the other way."

She pulled one foot up on the seat and turned toward me with an arm around her knee. "Are you going to lecture me about sexuality? Because you're a man who doesn't have relationships with women unless there's money and a contract behind it."

"Not true."

"When was the last time you were with a woman without the security of it being an escort transaction?"

"I couldn't tell you."

She nodded and sat back. "Exactly. So, like I said, we're both unhealthy and unavailable. Stop pressuring me and let me go. You won't see me again because it hurts too much to see Blue and leave him."

It hurt us both to see her and leave her. "I'd really like to take that pain away from you."

"And we've just covered all the reasons you can't. I have to live with it. Take me back to the hotel."

We were at an impasse. She wasn't budging. Her reasons were bullshit but that's what she was giving me right now. She'd closed down and was hiding. "There were so many things I wanted to do to you."

"Please stop," she whispered and I thought she might cry, but she bit her lip and held it in.

We were back where we'd started. Screw that. I absolutely hated going round and round and ending up nowhere. Just like my mom. Every time my dad left and came back, she took him, got pregnant, and added to the problem. In the end, I was the one who ended it. She didn't rescue us or herself. She blamed me for his death and made me doubt myself. It wasn't guilt. It was giving everything to someone who didn't want it and being left with nothing in the end. I swore I wouldn't put me or my family in that situation ever again.

I never surrendered, but this was a battle I couldn't win without her on my side.

"All right. You've proven your case." I started up the car, rolled up the windows, and drove her back to the Hotel Del.

Chapter 27 All In

Kissing her goodbye again sucked.

I'd told her I wanted to kiss her hello instead.

No dice.

I'd walked away, leaving her alone and on the verge of tears. I drove back to the beach with a confused and fidgety Blue in tow. He missed her too. Blasting the music didn't silence the urge to drive back there and take her anyway. I'd finally found a woman I want to be mine, and she had a long list of why we could never be together.

I parked the car and took off heading south with Blue. We both needed to run like we needed to breathe. Blue pulled the entire time like a sled dog because that's who he was. I kept the tension tight to make it more challenging because that's who I was.

We ran forever. Down the same beaches I ran during BUD/S. When the rocks jutted out into the water, we climbed or swam, but we didn't stop and had no plans to run back in the other direction. Just like my nightmare, running away from where I really wanted to be.

When I saw the markers for the Mexican border patrol, we had to stop. They wouldn't let us run through there and we needed to turn back anyway. We stopped to get some water out of a spigot at a campground. We'd run at least ten miles without stopping. We sat in the shade for a minute to recharge. His tongue hanging out to the side, he loved it. So did I. My legs ached and my lungs burned, but I was accustomed to abusing myself. I fought my demons like this. They often won, but I didn't know any other way to fight.

We ran back at a slower pace, my brain finally open to looking at this with something slightly more reasonable than full-scale rage.

In the end, it all boiled down to one thing. I couldn't force her to risk everything to leave the Agency for me. She had to choose it.

Just like I couldn't persuade a man to become a SEAL. You have to want it in your soul. It has to be who you're meant to be or you'll drop out the first time the ocean kicks your ass.

Blue and I returned to the yacht worn out, sweaty, and no less agonized over leaving our girl behind. Axel, Magnum, Teague, Talon, and London were sitting out on the deck, drinking beer and lounging in the sun.

I tossed my keys and grabbed a water. "What's the occasion?"

"You're fucking a Russian spy," Axel said with a smirk.

"I'm not fucking her."

"Bullshit. We all heard everything today," Magnum said.

"You heard nothing."

"We planted a bug in her purse." Teague grinned like it was his idea. Bastard. "Did you know she was packing a .45 in there?"

"Fuck you guys."

"I want you to defect for me, Kroshka." Magnum mocked me.

"Oh, we heard it all right," Axel chimed in. "I love your big schlongski, Viper." He imitated a female voice.

"She didn't say that. She said I have an incredible cock," I tipped my water toward him, "which is true."

Magnum sputtered his beer and laughed.

"Seriously, dude. What's up?" Teague asked.

"She came here under the pretenses of using me for sex, and I obliged."

"And what's really happening?"

"The SVG has hooks into her but she wants out. She's using me as a symbol of the possibilities to work through all that."

"I think you're her mark." Talon spoke for the first time. I had no idea he'd been developing this opinion of her, but I didn't like that he thought the worst of her.

"I'm not, but what if I am? What's she got on me?"

"She has control of your dick," Talon said. "You're compromised."

He was repeating what I'd said in Colombia. Fair enough. I did feel that way back then. Now things were different.

"She knows I'm a former SEAL, but that was obvious, nothing else. No contact info, no last names. She's not a threat."

"She's working you." Talon wasn't dropping this.

"What does she think she's gonna get? I'm not telling her shit about the teams or Knight Security. Anything I do tell her is intentional so she brings that information home to her handler. That we're the best out there, and they don't want to take us on for whatever perceived benefit they think there might be to Russia right now, which there is none."

"I say we follow her. If nothing else to see what she tells the handler, but I'd like to make sure she's safe." Teague's interest in her surprised me. He hadn't mentioned her in the months since his rescue, and he'd claimed he'd told me everything.

Which reminded me of something I'd been meaning to ask him. "Did you give her the website url and password?" Who else would do something like that? Only my brother who was locked in a cell with her for several hours and took care of her injured back.

"I may have slipped her a note when I shook her hand." He sat back in his chair acting casual, but he'd created a path for her to contact me, which also created contact with him.

"Teague, need to talk to you alone about this."

"Nope." Magnum stood up. "We all heard what she's been through. That shit is whacked. We're all invested now. Not just you."

Why did all these guys think they could save the girl when I couldn't?

"Okay. You're invested? Let me lay it out for you. I tried to get my mom out for years. It got so bad we were living in the Bush eating beavers and fighting off bears." I pointed to my scar to remind them. "Teague got Lyme's Disease. He was so weak he almost died. Still she went back to him when he came into town. He'd apologize or threaten her with whatever bullshit he was using. He tried to kill my sister, and I shot him with my shotgun. My mom blamed me for his death." I turned my gaze to Teague, but he was looking at the deck. I wasn't sure who on the team had heard the story about my dad, but they all knew now. "I care about Misha, okay? I admit it. She's got me fucking upside down. If she gives the word, I'm there in a shot, but I gotta learn from my mistakes. I can't put us all out there like that for her if she's gonna keep going back."

Everyone sat quietly for a second and turned their attention to their beer. They were starting to get it now.

Teague spoke first. "I have the same mother, and it makes me want to help Misha more."

How in the hell could we both have the same experience and come up with such different reactions to it? I opened my mouth to tell him that was because I shielded him from the worst of it, but a female voice speaking Russian came out into the air between us. "That's her," I said.

"What's she saying?"Axel held up a monitor screen with a speaker.

"If you'd shut up I could listen and tell you."

Misha spoke efficiently with a male who also spoke in Russian. The call ended abruptly.

"She set up a meeting with him tonight at six at a restaurant downtown." I looked at my men, each one in turn. "She said she has something she needs to tell him."

"Is this guy she's meeting the same one that picked her up at the airport?" London asked.

"Most likely." My skin itched at the thought of her hugging him like she had last time.

"Is he a threat?" Axel asked.

"I think he's her handler. He doesn't protect her." God, I wanted to kill that asshole.

Magnum sat forward. "We set up surveillance and roll to her meeting. After that, we call in Auggie." He looked at me.

August "Auggie" Provotorova was former Russian KGB turned Navy SEAL turned Knight operator.

"We won't need Auggie," I said.

"He would have the inside scoop on the SVG. If she wants out and we're helping her, we'll need his advantage."

Magnum was missing a key factor here. "We can't help her unless she wants it. Believe me, I've tried to find another way. She has to make the leap."

Magnum shook his head. "Ten-to-one she's going to tell him she wants out, and we end up fighting for her. If you're that hooked on her, she's double that hooked on you. She's already proven herself by leading us to Teague. I say we shadow her tonight and call in Auggie to help with the rest." Magnum was also saying he was all in.

This was a huge step because we'd be taking an active stance with her against the SVG and this Sergei person.

"You all need to understand the risks. We could be accused of conspiring with a foreign agent." It also meant putting myself out there to be rejected yet again. "But if Magnum's correct and she plans to talk to her handler about getting out, she'll need backup if things go south."

"Since when are we afraid of anything?" London said. "Either we're all in or no go. I think she wants out, and she could be an asset on our side over there. It's hard to infiltrate the SVG."

Talon grinned for the first time tonight. "Like a double agent? How incredible is that cock of yours? You think you can get her to do it?"

"I can't convince her to do anything." I'd accepted that.

"If the feds find out about this, we say we're investigating her. She's a person of interest, possibly open to flipping for us." Talon saying this meant he'd changed his stance and now he supported following her.

Could this really be happening? She was ready and needed me there? If so, I wouldn't let her down.

"You want her, V?" Teague asked me.

"More than anything," I admitted.

"She sacrificed herself for me. They burned her back." Teague spoke quietly, but landed that punch to my gut.

"I'm more than aware." I nodded and sat down. They got me. I was one hundred percent on-board with this.

"Then we're all in." Teague smiled, happy he'd won.

Now that the team had set it as a goal, there was no other option.

"Call up Jade, Shadow, and Locke," I said to Axel. "Get their asses here ASAP. I'll talk to Auggie myself. It's go time."

Chapter 28 Sacrifice

Misha

If there was such a thing as mustering grit like Steel had said, I was going to need to do it tonight.

Kiri would not be happy about what I had to say, so I'd set up the meeting in a public place where he'd be forced to maintain his composure.

In the lobby of the restaurant downtown, he kissed my cheek, and I tilted my chin to accept it.

As we followed the waitress to a table on the patio, I could think of nothing but Vander. It broke my heart to let him leave, but I needed to do this on my own. I couldn't drag him further into the deadly web of Sergei and the SVG, but I also couldn't resume my post and return to feeling dead inside when I'd only just felt alive for the first time.

"You didn't return my calls." Kiri leaned forward and whispered with his elbows on the table.

"You really need to get a hobby. Keeping tabs on me has to be boring." I opened my napkin on my lap, pretending to be collected when I was really falling apart inside.

"I'm responsible for you."

"Not officially. This is something you choose to do." He wasn't my official handler although he spent so much time with me, he'd taken on the role defacto.

"I care about you." He sounded genuine, but I couldn't tell if he meant it or not.

"Do you really? Or are you watching out for your own back?"

He growled and looked away. My brother and I had this complex relationship of needing each other because of our situation but also desperately wanting independence from each other. It was a constant struggle.

"So, how have you been?" I sat back and opened up the menu, ignoring the fierce anger rolling off him.

"I've been going through hell in Colombia dealing with the fallout of your actions."

"That was unnecessary." I was done with Colombia forever. He couldn't change that.

"You're back in good standing with Ruben Duran. I've convinced him the Americans pressured you to confess. The mission is still active. Your orders were to wait for my signal then return to Duran's side and yet you came here? Why?"

I didn't want to tell him anything that would put Vander at risk, but I did feel obligated to provide some explanation to my brother who had been there for me many times throughout the years. "I had a personal need."

"Have you lost your mind? I just sold my kidneys to get you back in there and you disappear to the States. It's suicide."

"I'd rather die than go back." It was true. I was done worrying about getting killed and ready to just let it finally happen. If I acted completely on my own, hopefully, they wouldn't retaliate on Kiri too.

He dropped his menu and glared at me. "You what?" His nostrils flared and he stood up. "Let's take this outside."

"No lunch?"

"Shut up. Outside. Now." I knew he'd be mad, but I'd made up my mind on this and couldn't be swayed. My life had to change now, or I couldn't keep on living.

I followed him out into the alley behind the restaurant. We were between brick buildings on both sides and the alley was empty.

He stopped walking and spun on me. "Who's making you talk crazy like this?"

"No one."

"You would never do this alone. One of those Navy SEALs?"

"How did you know they were SEALs?" The more Kiri knew, the more danger Vander and his team were in. I hated this mess I'd created for everyone around me.

"Duran had extracted it from his prisoner. They were Navy SEALs. He thinks one of the guys was his brother. Is that true?"

"I can't tell you anything." I'd never betray Vander, even to save my own brother.

"What the hell is wrong with you? Tell me everything right now. You're gonna get us all killed just so you can get laid by some sailor you got the hots for?"

"No!" Talking about it was making it all so much worse. Tears welled in my eyes. "Listen. If I act alone, no one will pay. Not you. Not him. I can save you both." This wasn't how I planned to present it to him, but my emotions were talking now.

"You're crying for him? Are you in love with him?" He sneered like he was asking me if I had done something disgusting.

"I didn't intend to fall in love."

"But you did?"

Yes. "It doesn't matter."

"You're in love with a Navy SEAL and you can't tell me anything and it doesn't matter? This is the bullshit you're feeding me?"

"I ended it. It's over. I'll go to Sergei myself and tell him I want out."

"Has anyone ever just waltzed in there and walked out alive? No. He'll kill you like he did our parents and Alvaro."

His mention of Alvaro sent a shiver down my spine. The only man I'd ever considered loving was dead before it could start. "Please try to understand."

He gripped my upper arms and shook me. "They'll kill us both. Don't you understand?"

I didn't fight back and let him shake me like a rag doll. I'd given up. This body meant nothing to me anymore. "I'd rather be dead than let Duran touch me again."

Kiri stared into my eyes, confused, angry, concerned. I understood what I was saying would end both our lives as we knew it, but it was time for drastic change. We couldn't go on like this.

"I'll pay for this. Not you. And it'll be worth it." I tried to reassure him of something I didn't know myself.

"No it won't. Not if you're dead."

"I wasn't meant to be this woman," I said quietly.

"Dammit, Misha." He punched the wall of the building behind me.

"I can't fall in line any longer."

Rapid footsteps came running around the corner of the alley. Three men barrelled toward us, Vander in the front, his lips set forward in ultra-focused determination.

Kiri braced for their attack and started swinging at Vander. The other two men stopped on either side of us and watched Vander and my brother collide in the alley. They exchanged punches, but Vander forced Kiri to the ground with a hammer fist to the back of his neck. Vander pinned him on his stomach. Kiri jabbed his elbow into Vander's side and kicked the heel of his boot into his back.

I'd tried this before with Vander. It didn't work. He was built like a brick house. Ankles and elbows would never take him down. You had to get him by the neck or the balls, and he'd never let his guard down long enough for that to happen.

"You hit a woman, you coward." Vander punched his face and I cringed. I hated to see them fighting like this.

"I didn't hit her. I hit the wall behind her head, you moron."

Vander was breathing heavily as he got up and let Kiri rise. They eyed each other like they were eager to go a second round. "You fight like her? You look like her?" Vander squinted as he scrutinized Kiri closely. "You're her brother?"

"Fuck you," Kiri spat back.

"You don't protect her? You let them control her?" He stepped closer to Kiri with his fists up, ready to throw down with him again.

"Van," I pleaded for him to stop.

"No. Fuck this. He's your brother? He stands by and allows them to violate you time after time?"

"I do not." Kiri pulled his shoulders back, but he was roughed up from the fight.

"You've seen the scars on her back? They poured boiling water on her. You're not taking responsibility for that? You're attacking her in an alley instead of getting her safe?"

Oh my gosh. Vander standing up for me stirred all kinds of emotions in my heart. It reminded me of the day he stood in front of me when we arrived at the handoff. My entire life, no one had shielded me. Not my father, not Sergei, not Kiri. And Vander was honorably doing it again.

"You don't understand what you're saying," Kiri replied.

"I do. I've seen this a million times. You're no better than them for standing by. Whether she fights it or not. You stand by and let it happen until her soul is drained dry and she has no more fight in her."

"Vander." I tried to interrupt, but he wasn't listening to me.

"Why don't we take you in and pour boiling water on your back and see how she reacts? You think she wouldn't give her life for you? She sacrificed herself for my goddamn brother. She'd probably do anything for you, and you do shit to help her."

Kiri looked down and spoke softly. "I've done all I can."

"Bullshit. If you'd done all you could, she'd be free, she wouldn't have scars on her back or her soul. She'd be busy worrying about what movie to watch at night, not being tortured or running for her life."

Kiri wiped his forehead and smoothed down his hair. He turned his attention on me. "He knows too much, Misha."

"No, he doesn't," I replied.

"He's a risk." Kiri was taking this route to get to me. He knew if Vander was in jeopardy, I'd give up my fight, but once again, Vander shielded me.

"You're at risk of getting your face bashed in in the next five seconds if you don't leave here right now."

"Let's go, Misha."

"She's not leaving with you."

Kiri looked to me for my answer. I made eye contact with Vander. The honor, love, and compassion I saw there told me all I needed to know. "I'm not leaving with you this time, Kiri. I'm sorry."

"You can't be serious."

"Please, just let me handle this. For all we've shared and all we've been through, I'm asking you to give me a chance to work this out on my own."

Kiri nodded like he was finally accepting it. "I won't abandon you, Misha. I'll give you some space to figure out where your head is at but you're not walking in there and turning yourself over to Sergei. I won't allow it."

I nodded. I'd have to find another way that wouldn't put him or Vander in danger.

"This is a test," Vander said to Kiri with a threatening tone. "Cover for her. If anyone shows up here looking for her, we'll know you betrayed her."

Kiri sneered at Vander and lifted his chin at me before he turned his back and walked away.

Vander took my hand in a tight grip, and his shoulders were stiff as he marched in the opposite direction as Kiri. In all the chaos, I hadn't realized the two men standing there watching everything were Steel and Magnum. I wanted to say hello, but no one was smiling or talking and another group of very large men and one woman were striding toward us.

Vander stopped and waited for them to reach us. No one had weapons drawn, but I had the strong feeling they were all heavily armed. "Follow him. Rally at my place tomorrow morning." Vander gave orders with absolute authority. In other words, we're not talking now. We'll talk later.

The team seemed to expect this or understand because they all peeled off in different directions. The entire interaction lasted less than ten seconds.

We reached his car, and he opened the door for me stiffly. I sat down and he slammed the door, stalked around the front to his side, got in, and sat silently without starting the engine.

"You were listening?" I asked him.

He chewed his lip and stared out the windshield. "I heard everything."

"Including the part about..."

"Loving me? Yeah." He jammed the key into the ignition, and the car rumbled to life.

He checked his side mirror and pulled away from the curb. He didn't say anything else. He didn't need to. His silence and his clenched jaw said it all.

Every stoplight made him more impatient. He tapped the wheel with his index finger and ground his teeth so fiercely I could hear a crunch.

After a short ride, we pulled into the Hotel del Coronado parking lot. He left the car idling as he draped one of his big muscular arms behind my seat and turned to lean into me.

"You lied to Duran so he would arrest you and lead you to Steel." His voice was deep, raspy, and serious.

I wasn't sure how this related to what just happened, but I answered, "Yes. You know this."

"Duran's men poured boiling water on your back to get intel on me, and you didn't give it up?"

"No, because they would come for you."

"The SVG questioned you, and you told them nothing?"

Oh. I saw where he was going. "No," I said quietly.

"You sacrificed so much for me." His eyes softened and filled with pain. I didn't know my actions would hurt him. I was trying to help.

"Yes. So you could be with your brother who loves you. What good would it do to reunite you then have you tracked down and killed?"

"Right."

He turned off the engine, climbed out, and walked around to my side to open the door. He still seemed angry, but at least his teeth weren't grinding anymore. We took the elevator up to the third floor and exited toward my room. "Gather all your belongings." He closed the door behind him as soon as we were in the room. "You're staying with me to keep you safe."

"Kiri won't betray me."

"That remains to be seen."

"I know he won't."

"Gather all your things. We can't talk here."

"Why are you so angry?"

"He's your brother. He should protect you. Get your stuff."

I was still confused as I collected my clothes and my bags. He said he was mad at Kiri, but I was the one feeling all the anger and heat from his body. By the time I was finished, he'd cooled a little. "You got everything?"

"Yes."

"Good."

His dispassionate gaze threw me off. I never thought he'd find out how I really felt about him, but now that he had, I expected some sort of reaction. Kiss me, yell at me, but don't give me the cold shoulder. Just like the first night I met him and the day after we had sex the first time, he pushed me away and didn't talk to me. He was doing it again, pulling away when I penetrated the walls of his iceberg.

Chapter 29 We Can't Fall in Love

Vander

Blue greeted her with the fire of a thousand suns. She dropped to her knees to enjoy the kiss-fest. "I missed you, baby boy," she cooed.

Seeing her with Blue helped take the edge off the anger toward Kiri. She thought I was mad at her, but I really wanted to kill him, and she caught me in a rough spot as I tried to work through it.

If I killed the asshole, he would never come back to harm her. Problem solved. Of course, she would be upset if I killed her brother, so I was forced to let him live. I couldn't tell her I was struggling with the fact I let her brother live, so I had to try to hide it, which made this all fucked up beyond repair. I threw my gear and her bag on the floor by my bedroom door.

"This is where you live?" She checked out the living room and peeked down the hallway of my apartment. It was an upscale place with a killer view of downtown and the harbor from the thirty-third floor.

"You're surprised?"

"I guess I expected you to live in a bunker with your face painted green and leaves on your head."

"Huh, no." I chuckled. "This building has top-notch security and trustworthy management. The other guys have apartments on the same floor."

Well, look at that. I spoke in a normal tone like I had regained control of myself. Her gorgeous lips tilted up in an approving smile and my dick twitched. She hadn't sucked my cock yet. I should throw her to the floor and fuck her face while I ate her...

Okay, definitely not in control yet. Not the way I needed to be to handle her and this delicate situation correctly. Rushing her right now and fucking her raw on the floor would not solve any of our problems.

She looked up at me with big doe eyes that said she would absolutely be open to fucking on the floor right now. "I need a drink."

I turned away from her beautiful face, and she followed me into the kitchen. The tumblers clinked together and the ice plunked into the bucket as I fumbled around, not sure if I wanted to kill or fuck or fight. I didn't know who I was. "Gin all right?"

"Yes."

I grabbed a bottle of Hendrick's and cracked the seal open. I took a swig straight from the bottle, and she grinned as I hissed through the burn.

"You seem a little nervous."

"And you seem to be enjoying that."

She laughed. "I am. It's a rare treat."

"I wanted to kill him." I blurted it out. God, I had to get my shit together or this woman would think I was insane.

"Kiri?"

"Yeah. I didn't because he's your brother."

"Well, that's good. I'm glad you didn't kill my only living relative. Is that why you're drinking from the bottle?"

"Yes. I'm working through it."

"It's not about... what you overheard?"

"Nope." I picked up my ice, tumblers, and gin and walked out to the balcony. I placed the stuff on the outdoor bar and started working on the drinks. She stepped back and leaned against the railing of the balcony to watch me.

In her glass, I put a lot of ice, figuring she wasn't used to drinking gin.

I dropped two ice cubes in my glass and poured the clear liquid into both tumblers. I forced myself to focus on the salt in the air and the marine layer rolling in. I'd been acting like an ass. She'd put herself out there, and I wasn't handling it well.

I pushed the idea of killing her brother out of my mind and looked into her eyes. Time to ease some of the worry I saw there.

Holding the two glasses in my hands, I turned toward her. "There's this girl I know."

She stood up a little straighter. "Oh really?"

"A full-grown woman actually. You should see her in action. Gorgeous body that moves like a high-performance race car, smart like a fox, good with a gun. Really my dream girl."

"Hmm." Her gaze dropped down to the drinks in my hand.

"And she told me we couldn't fall in love."

Her pretty brown eyes rose up to mine again. "Did she now?"

"Gave me a long list of reasons." I took a slow step closer, stalking her.

She shifted her weight and looked out at the view. "That was silly of her. Who wouldn't want to fall in love with you?"

"That's what I was wondering. She said I lacked compassion, but she didn't know I was the one who had the idea to buy her a dog to ease her night terrors." With each step closer, I could feel her pull. We were drawn together like planets in orbit.

"Oh, how thoughtful of you."

"She said I had a hero complex, but the truth is she really needed a strong man to motivate her to make things right in her life."

Her chest heaved with her deep breaths. Her eyes seduced me as they locked onto my lips. "Yes, sometimes we all need that extra push."

"We're screwed up in the same ways—me and this woman. We understand each other. We've both lived life on the edge, pretending to be someone else, seeking action instead of facing who we are." I came within a foot of her, and her nipples pebbled under her blouse.

"She sounds perfect for you. Too bad she had so many reasons."

I reached her and stood with our bodies a hair's breadth apart, the electromagnetic force between us so strong, I couldn't fight it. "You know what I do when someone tells me I can't do something?" My skin sizzled from being this close to her, even fully clothed.

"Oh no."

I leaned down and whispered in her ear, "I set my mind to it and refuse to give up until it's done."

"Vander..." She shivered from head to toe, her breathing ragged, her head tilting ever so slightly to give me more access to her neck.

"Try to talk me out of it, I'll work harder to get it." I pressed my lips below her ear, holding the drinks between us. She whimpered and my dick thickened. We hadn't even touched yet, and she had me weak in my knees ready to burst out of my pants.

"Please don't toy with my bitter heart."

"Turns out." I spoke as I kissed a trail down the supple skin of her neck. "She was in love with me the entire time. She was just looking for excuses cuz she was scared."

She laughed nervously and her hands came up to grip my waist, kneading the loops of my pants desperately like she couldn't wait to get them off. Me too, darling. Me too. "What a silly woman."

I pulled away and looked her straight in the eye. "So, I'm going for it. I'm gonna let her know I love her too."

She gasped, her face locked in cute shock. I pressed my lips to her cheek and inhaled her feminine scent.

"You think she'll have me?" God, I loved seeing her speechless like this. Tongue-tied and twisted, her shoulders stiff and nervous while her body was begging me to touch her.

"I think she'd be crazy not to." Her breathless voice went straight to my cock, which I pressed against her belly and she pushed back, smashing my dick between us. I held back my groan, not wanting to reveal how much she had affected me already.

"That's good because this woman and I have rockin' sex, and I want more of it."

"I heard there were things you wanted to do to her." Her hands tickled up my chest, and her palms warmed my skin as they landed flat on my pecs. Just that small touch from her made me weak. She was taking advantage of the fact my hands were occupied.

"So many things. I already gave her the shaken-and-stirred-with-a-twist-of-danger package." I slipped my tongue in her mouth and the sweet taste of her had me struggling to hold back.

She ended the kiss and hummed against my lips. "Mmm. I bet she loved that."

"She did. Came long and hard on my cock."

"Vander." Her hand slid down and palmed my dick. I thought I'd explode right there. She literally had me in the palm of her hand, and I liked being there.

"Tonight she's getting the on-the-rocks package."

"And what does that include?" Her eyes were half-closed, her mouth open, totally receptive to whatever I wanted to give her.

"It includes a long slow torture that'll break down the last of the ice wall between us." I skimmed one of the cold glasses over her nipple through her blouse. She gasped and arched away. I'd shocked her out of her dreamlike state. Her hands came off my body, and she narrowed her eyes. I tipped my head, daring her to stop me.

Slowly, she braced her elbows back on the railing, opening her chest and offering her tits up for more cold treatment. I grazed the other glass on her other nipple, this time rubbing the hard nub with my knuckle. Her mouth dropped fully open, and a sexy sigh came from the back of her throat. Her back was still tense though. I almost had her full submission to this. I scraped my teeth along her jaw as I spoke in a soft murmur. "I'll chip away at it with each bite of my teeth, each kiss of her skin." I wanted to eat her alive right now, but that would ruin all the fun.

"Sounds fantastic. I wish I were that lucky woman."

"You can be. Just open your legs."

Chapter 30 Hot Ice

She paused and looked into my eyes for reassurance, testing to see if I meant it. I nodded, encouraging her to play along. "C'mon, baby. Spread your legs for me."

She did as I asked and pride surged through me. Her thighs and calves pulled taut, and she looked fucking delectable in her heels and short skirt. My sexy Russian spy was offering herself to me, and I could not have been more pleased.

"Wider. Till your skirt is up."

She stepped out further and brought her hands down to slide her skirt up over her luscious curvy hips, revealing light pink lace over her silky pussy. Fuck me. Holy shit, she was like every centerfold I'd ever masturbated over and every beauty queen rolled into one alluring package.

"Good girl. Keep your elbows back." I reached up and poured a few drops of ice-cold gin into her mouth. A trickle dribbled off the bottom of the cup and down the side of my hand. She licked her lips and purred as she swallowed. "You have got to be the most exquisite creation I've ever seen. Your legs spread for me, nipples hard, hot pussy on display, mouth open. A feast for my senses."

I took a sip of my own drink and placed the glasses on the railing behind her. As I kissed her, and the liquid sloshed around in our mouths, I fished an ice cube out of the glass and pressed it to her core between her legs. She gasped, but I didn't release her mouth. I wanted to inhale her every moan, every breath, every vibration I caused in her body.

With my other hand, I swiped another ice cube and pressed it to her nipple over her clothes. She shivered and pulled back.

We both tensed and didn't move. I was giving her another chance to back out of this but seriously hoping she wouldn't.

Yes! My girl arched her back and offered me her chest. "God, I love that you aren't giving up. You want me to keep going. You're not afraid. Toughing it out. Trusting me." I swirled both ice cubes in slow circles on her nipples until the fabric was wet and I could see her mesmerizing red nubs begging to be warmed by my hot mouth. She had the most tempting breasts, even more mouth watering with her nipples cold and hard from my torture. The wetter it got, the more she had to be feeling it. My fingertips burned from the cold, so I knew she must be uncomfortable. She sucked in a long stuttered breath through her teeth.

"Trust me, babe. This will be totally worth it in the end."

I placed both ice cubes, that were now getting smaller, in my mouth and kissed her. Her body tightened and she dove into the kiss, her tongue and mine fighting for control while playing with the ice in my mouth. As she became engrossed in the kiss, I worked patiently on unbuttoning her blouse, unhooking her bra, and freeing her tantalizing tits to the air. Goosebumps surrounded her pebbled buds. I pulled one between my lips and teased it with the ice.

"God!" Her body shook, and I gripped her ribs to hold her up.

"Elbows on the railing."

She dutifully pulled her arms back into position, and I rewarded her by switching to the other nipple and plucking it with my teeth. She moaned and shivered, but didn't try to stop me.

Keeping her distracted by my mouth working her tit, I snaked another ice cube from the glass behind her and slowly slid it down her flat stomach into the front of her panties. Her legs trembled when the ice hit her clit. I circled it there for a long time, getting it nice and cold so when my hot mouth hit it, she'd feel double the sensation.

The ice in my mouth melted, and she moaned as I swallowed around her nipple. I kept playing it with my tongue, and it all started to warm up.

"Oh." She gripped my head and pulled it tight to her tit.

Yeah, now she was getting it.

I could probably make her come from just this, but I didn't want to. I wanted my cock in her tight pussy when she came so I could feel it and draw it out forever.

I worked the ice cube down between her folds and raised my head to kiss her as I slid it inside. "You good, babe?"

She grabbed my face and devoured me with her thrusting tongue. I answered her back with equal greed. Oh yeah. I needed to fuck her right now. I needed to push inside her and thrust, thrust, thrust until she couldn't see straight and we both came hard.

But that wasn't what she needed, so I forced myself to lower the intensity of the kiss and went for another ice cube. She whimpered into my mouth as I brushed the ice over her nipple, trailed it down her soft navel, and slid it inside her now-soaked panties.

She squirmed to get away but I pressed her hips back against the wall and held her still. "Take it."

She groaned and threw her head back, only making me want to tease her longer with faster, tighter swipes at her clit with the hard ice cube.

Slowly, I worked four cubes inside her and swallowed every one of the little mewls coming from the back of her throat. So sexy. While I was busy with my little task, she managed to peel off my shirt and unbuckle my pants. She freed my dick and tugged hard. We were both in a frantic rush to ease the cold and bring on the heat that would send her over the edge.

I grinned at her as I added two new ice cubes to my mouth. With a quick strike, she jammed her tongue inside and deftly stole them into her own. Once again, I'd underestimated her, assuming she'd keep taking whatever I gave her. Who was the viper now?

She slid to her knees, pulling my pants and briefs all the way down to my ankles. I held my breath, anticipating the unfathomable cold that would hit me when she sucked my dick. But she surprised me by going lower, deeper, and wrapping chilled lips around my balls and pressing the ice right up against my sensitive skin.

Shards of frost raced up my spine. I arched my back, trying to adjust to the overwhelming sight of her lips on my balls and the cold that burned and felt fantastic at the same time. She twirled the ice around ruthlessly and gave me a new appreciation of the term blue balls.

"Fuck."

She giggled and said, "Take it," in a garbled laugh. She removed her mouth and replaced it with her warm hands, and I rapidly understood what she must've felt on her nipples. The warming sensation was absolutely intense and hit me hard just as her icy lips sank onto the crown of my dick. She pushed deep, sucking all the way down my shaft, the ice burning holes into my dick as she swirled it around.

I was about to give up control to her and let her ice my dick till it was numb and suck it like a popsicle, but shit, the point of this was her, not me.

"Enough." I pulled her up by her armpits and kissed her. She laughed like the naughty girl she was. I yanked her panties off and smashed my huge cold hard dick between her legs. That stopped her laughter instantly. We both knew relief and ecstasy were waiting in the wings as soon as we generated enough heat to defrost our frozen parts. "Want to feel this without a condom, babe."

"Yes." She wrapped a leg over my hip and tilted her pelvis, urging me to take it. "Now."

Following orders, I rammed my hard, cold cock inside her. It felt like diving naked into snow. The frigid water spilled out of her pussy and down her legs. She was full-on shaking now from head to toe.

"Brace yourself, babe. I'm gonna warm you up fast, and it's gonna blow your mind."

"Yes, God. Hurry. So cold."

I realized now that I'd been holding back with her before. This time, I could finally selfishly take from her, plunder her, own her. I still needed to hear her say it. "I want to smash into you, push you, break you." I growled the words through gritted teeth and a clenched jaw.

She nodded impatiently. "Yes. Everything you've got. All of you. Give it to me. Hard and fast."

Before she finished speaking, I slammed our bodies together and thrust into her brutal and swift. My chest crushed her naked tits, my groin smashed and swiveled on her clit, rubbing away the cold and generating something totally new.

Quickly, the friction between us caused the numbness to give way to the most excruciating, ultra-electric, satisfying tingle. It was that superheated pins and needles feeling you get when you put your icy toes up next to the fire, but magnified a thousand times because it was my cock and her pussy and we were ramming together like two sticks trying to generate a spark.

I kissed her and forced her back down to the railing to maximize contact. I wanted my dick lodged so deep inside her she'd feel it in her soul. She only had one foot on the ground and was almost horizontal, her knee squeezing my hip, clutching my ass to her as I held her up.

And then I felt it rising in her and that made it rise in me like magic rending its way from her sweet pussy into my dick. We were dancing on the verge of bursting into flames.

"Oh. I'm gonna... Van... It's like so..."

"I know, babe. Me too. I'm so close. Give me your eyes. I wanna see it in your eyes." My hand behind her neck forced her head up.

Yes, her burning gaze told me everything. She was a blazing inferno ready to blow. Our bodies slammed together in a spiraling rhythm, her tits bouncing, my other hand squeezing her ass, every inch of us connected in total resonance.

I kept pumping into her, no mercy, deeper than I thought possible, no concern if I was hurting her, not worried if I was hitting her clit or her G-spot, just primal rutting that came from somewhere deep in my soul, rubbing my dick against her slick walls in a savage insatiable attack.

"Fuck me. Fuck. Come for me, Kroshka. Come hard for me." I didn't even know what I was saying, I was so lost in her tight grip. I needed her to come so I could release this giant ache peaking in my balls.

A high-pitched keen and a breathless grunt escaped the back of her throat. She was about to come.

"Yes. Fuck."

She seized up and her whole body clenched around my dick so goddamn tight, hard like a vise clamping down over and over. I hissed through the overwhelming onslaught of it. Jesus, this woman would destroy me.

Her hot walls kept gripping me tight, milking me until I couldn't stave it off a second longer. It was right there. That blissful edge. I'd never felt such an unabiding need for release before.

It ripped and blasted from deep in my balls, shooting into her core while she was still pulsing through her orgasm. Ropes and ropes of endless come emptied into her, making the impossible inferno even hotter, even slicker, even more unbelievable. Time stopped and we hovered in unending nirvana.

As the tide eventually ebbed, my hips slowed, enjoying the easy stroke through the slick wetness where we were joined. Her eyes rolled back in her head as I kissed her lips, her chin, her chest, her tits. I pulled her up so she was vertical again and her head flopped to my shoulder. "Good job, babe. So good." She'd given her whole self to me and I'd taken it all. "Worth the wait?" I asked her.

"Absolutely."

I picked her up and she wrapped her legs around my waist as I carried her to my shower. We peeled off the rest of our wet clothes and I guided her under the hot waterfall. She grinned a lazy smile as the warm water ran down her back.

I stood behind her and kissed her scars. "Too hot? Too cold?" I didn't know if her scars were sensitive to temperature or not. I did know her nipples and pussy were very sensitive. I laughed to myself.

"It's fine. Everything is just fine."

Ha! I loved her like this. Easy, soft, pliable. Finally my hellcat was a mewling kitten.

"Don't tell anyone, but you're my dream woman."

She smiled and I turned her chin back so I could draw long kisses from her sated mouth. My dick started to fill and I wanted to take her again in my shower like I'd imagined night after night when I jacked off thinking of her, but there would be more chances for us. Many more now that my Kroshka was officially mine.

Chapter 31 Details

Misha

I could get used to this whole having sex until you passed out and slept peacefully thing. So different from the constant angst and fear of being tracked or found out. I woke to Vander's deep voice echoing from the living room. Last night after our mind-boggling sex, I'd decided to show him my sketchbook today.

We'd gone from strangers to lovers in such a short time, and the whole confession of love thing was forced by Kiri pressuring me. He'd hinted that he loved me too last night, but that was before we had sex. You can never trust what a man says before sex.

Either way, I wanted to give Vander a chance to beg out. Until he knew the depth of my transgressions, he couldn't truly love me. He also had the right to know before he committed his heart to a cold-blooded murderer.

The sketches documented more than my crimes. All my life, the words I couldn't share with anyone, I drew. Maybe deep in my subconscious I always hoped I'd have someone to share my life with. If there was ever going to be the right time, now was it.

I clutched the sketchbook to my chest and stood in the bedroom doorway. Blue ran over to greet me. Vander turned, his eyes scanned me wearing his T-shirt from last night, and he grinned as he held his phone to his ear. He curled his fingers for me to come closer. I walked to him, and he pulled me onto his lap as I petted Blue on the head.

"Right. Later." He ended the call and turned his face up to mine. He planted a gentle kiss on my lips. "Mornin'."

"Good morning."

"I'll never get tired of watching you wake up in my T-shirt, walk over to me, and sit in my lap. If you did only that every day for the rest of my life, I'd be a happy man."

I laughed. "You're easy to please then."

"Hardly. What's this?"

He nodded at my hands running absently over the cover of my sketchbook.

"Do we have time to talk?"

"I always have time for you. The team will be here in an hour to discuss a plan to get you out of the Agency."

My blood ran cold at the thought of crossing Sergei, but I'd set my mind to it and accepted I had no other choice for my life. These days with Vander only reinforced my decision. This is the woman I was meant to be. If I had to face death to break free, I would do what it took.

"Is it a notebook?" He brought my attention back to my sketchbook with its tattered edges and dirty pages.

"This is the only item in the world that is truly mine. I've protected it and kept it hidden my entire life. You're the first person to ever see it." If his team was coming over to talk about me, sharing this first was even more important. They all deserved to know what they were getting involved in.

He looked up at me and his eyes softened as his arm tightened around my back. "Show me."

The pages crackled as I flipped open the cover. Sharp pain squeezed my lungs, making it hard to breathe. My hands and legs began to shake.

His palm came up to my neck tugged my face close to his. "It's okay." He tapped his chest. "Safe."

I took a deep breath. Safe. Vander was safe. "I want you to know me. The good and the bad, and I think by showing you this, you'll be able to trust me."

"I already trust you, Kroshka."

I shook my head. "It's hard to describe. Just, if you see this, I promise you and your team can trust me."

He nodded and turned his gaze back to the book.

The first page was the oldest. I was nine or ten when I drew the blue puppy I'd found in the streets. I'd sketched him in pencil and used a crayon to make his fur blue.

"Goluboy schenok," Vander said.

"Yes."

The next one was a little girl clutching the puppy as she wailed—her face dirty and agonized. My heart felt like it would burst out of my chest.

It symbolized everything I'd been through. The loss of innocence and childhood. Valuable things stripped from me coldly when all I wanted to do was love that dog. "They didn't have to take him. I was still living at home. We could've fed him scraps. They did it to be cruel. To prove a point. We control your life. Don't get attached to anything."

He patted his knee and Blue came over to us. I rubbed his head and lost control of the thin hold I had on my emotions. I drew his nose up and leaned down to receive a wet doggie tongue to lick the salty tear from my cheek. "When you brought him to me, it changed everything. It opened floodgates long closed. Desires for love and hopes and dreams that I hadn't entertained in years. It was gut-wrenching to think of all the things that could never be mine."

"But I let you hold him. I didn't take him away." He flipped through several more pages of blue dogs. A pack in the snow, all of them blue except one. In that pack, the white dog was the outsider.

The sketches turned very dark after that—only black, gray, and red. My mother's blood pooled on the floor by her limp arm. The images burned in my brain and salt thrown in the wound because my dad had tricked me. "He'd told me it was an opportunity to serve my country, use my special skills, but within a year or two, I knew what he'd done. He'd betrayed me. But he was dead, so I had no one to hate. All I had was Kiri, who joined the Agency a year later to look after me. These are scraps of paper that I pasted into the book when I had to hide it and dig it up again."

After my dark teens, more images of blue puppies, healthy dogs on leashes, walking with their humans in a park. A brief period of hope in my life.

Then there was an image of a fat man's naked body as he lay dead in a bed, a knife through his heart. Blood on the sheets. "My first assassination."

"Jeez, babe." He leaned his head into my chest. "I remember my first kill too."

I nodded. "A morbid thing to have in common. I want you to know this about me. I seduced and killed this man in cold blood."

He grunted. "I sliced the throat of your guard five minutes before you started shooting at me."

"It's different."

"Is it?" His arm squeezed my waist, and my head swam with the intensity of this conversation. I needed some coffee and a lifetime to sort all this out.

"I don't know. You were working for the American military. This man was Russian Bratva. The Pakhan of the rival family still hunts me. No kill is ever clean. Each one tarnishes you for life."

"I'm tarnished too then." He shrugged like it was simple, but we both knew the guilt of taking a life weighed heavy on your soul for years and drove some people mad.

Next, he flipped through impressionist-style paintings of landscapes without people, without dogs, muted colors. "These are places where I stayed. Mostly in Europe. Nameless. Empty. Never stopping to see details." The water from the paint had furrowed the page and made the whole thing a lumpy blob. Symbolic of how my life was at the time.

A few charcoal drawings of Kiri as a young man. I did add color to his cheeks but not a smile to his face. My easy-going clown of a brother had become very serious and dour from his life with the Agency. I felt that as a loss too.

Then came the rainforests of Colombia. A wild parrot. A coffee shop. Another hopeful time when I arrived in Colombia and mistakenly thought my life would be my own.

"I've spent the last few years in South America pretending to be Colombian. I posed as Skyler Perez, an art dealer, to meet influential people in wealthy circles. I slept my way into Duran's inner circle of organized crime."

He growled and his body grew tense.

"Let's continue." I knew what was coming next.

He turned the page to the first drawing of him. He was on his belly on the floor of my villa, decked out in full gear, fierce determination and bravery on his face. The other men in the room were just black outlines, but he was drawn in detail, including his night vision goggles, protective helmet, and armored vest.

He paused for a long time and stared at it. He didn't say anything and I felt nervous. "Jade brought me paper and a pen." Now he knew I admired him from the first moment. The only truly detailed drawings in my sketchbook were of him.

"I allowed it. Thought it would be good to get you writing."

"If you ask people, they'll usually give you a pen and paper."

The next ones were a series of drawings of him in the room talking to me. Sometimes his face showed no emotion. Most of them showed his face softer and more compassionate. One with him smirking as he lifted a scrappy puppy who would eventually be named Blue.

I held my breath as he flipped the page slowly. The next one was a man and a woman on a chair, her thighs spread over his lap, his arms holding hers behind her back. Her mouth gaped open in ecstasy. He was mostly dressed, his face stern and serious, straining to hold back his true nature. I felt naked in front of him as he took in the details.

"This is phenomenal, babe."

I exhaled. Good. He liked them. It was so important he accepted this part of me and my adoration of him.

He flipped to one of Steel with a bruised face sitting on the prison floor. He flinched, and I could feel the pain coming from his heart. Then one of me in a cell. He kept getting angrier and tenser. Then he softened at the pictures of Blue with him.

Every day I drew him with Vander, imagining how they looked talking, playing fetch, sleeping in a bed together.

"I haven't had a chance to draw the yacht yet."

"You drew all this from memory?"

"Yes. I have vivid imagery in my head. Drawing helps to get it out. It's like erasing it from my mind."

"Does it work?"

"Sometimes a little. Sometimes not at all."

"But you still have nightmares about goluboy schenok?"

"Not when I'm with you."

He pulled my head down to plant another kiss on my lips. I loved kissing him. His scent, his strength, his gentleness. Everything about him made me want more.

"You heal a lot of things for me too," he whispered as he closed the book.

"I do? Like what?"

"Not really good at talking about emotions and stuff, but I'd be happy to show you our "neat" package." He buried his chin in my neck, the scruff tickling my skin.

"Tell me what I heal in you."

He ran his tongue over his teeth under his lip. "After that first night when you asked me to kill you and I promised I'd do it, I felt like shit. How did I become the kind of man that would treat a woman that way? Even if my brother's life was at stake, it wasn't your fault."

I placed my palm flat on his cheek. "How did I help you with this?"

"And then I found out how dire your situation was. You were suicidal. You needed help. I wanted to be the man who fought for you."

"You did that."

"I had to convince you that it was worth it to take a chance. That you deserved it, and you should be open to a future where someone loved you for who you were. I ended up realizing I should be open too."

"To me?"

"Yeah. To loving you. To the chance I could get hurt or I could hurt you by getting killed. My brothers and I always thought we'd be dead before age thirty, and here I am at thirty-six, still fighting. How old are you?"

"Thirty-two."

"We're both getting too old for this life. Anyway, I realized that I didn't want to die without knowing what it was like to love you. You were knocking so hard on the door of my heart, I opened it up and let you in, and I liked you there. It felt right. Like I'd been given this gift of something rare and valuable, and I didn't want to blow it." He gazed up at me with dark, warm eyes.

"Am I valuable to you?"

"Priceless." He kissed me. "I'll never be a domestic guy, but I don't think you're that kind of woman either."

"Correct."

"How about shaken-and-stirred-with-a-twist-of-danger? You down with that?"

"You know I am."

"Good. However it ends up looking, I want you to know, I'm balls-to-the-wall, full-throttle with you, babe. Like jumping out the back end of a plane, I'm committed to it, freefall, no chute, no matter how we land."

"Really? I feel honored to be the woman you chose to give your heart to. I'm balls-to-the-wall too. You have my entire heart forever, no matter how we land."

Chapter 32 Just a Nip

Our kiss was interrupted by a knock at the door. "Hold that thought." He lifted me off his lap and patted my behind. "Go get dressed. No one sees this ass but me."

In the bedroom, I dressed in a skirt and a blouse with matching heels. My normal uniform. I was looking forward to shopping for jeans and sweats for a change.

Vander had some really nice paintings of sled dogs in the snow on his walls. I'd have to ask him about them. What would it be like to visit the snow with Vander and Blue? They'd be so in their element there. Not humid like Colombia or sunny like California, but huge expanses of cold snow to play in and ride fast.

The thought of snow reminded me of the ice cubes last night, and I shivered. I quickly took care of my bathroom necessities and joined the group in the living room.

I recognized Jade, Magnum, Axel, Talon, and London. The other guys I may have seen once or twice, but never learned their names. Every single one of them was tall, badass, and gorgeous.

Seeing Steel again warmed my heart. His face had healed, he'd bulked up. His deep hug and pat on the back took me by surprise. He smelled good and seemed happy. So different from the shattered man I'd met in the prison. "Good to see you." His eyes lit up with a boyish smile.

"Good to see you too, Steel." I blushed at this direct attention from Vander's brother. We'd shared a lot and I felt my own special connection to him, but I didn't realize he may have felt it too. I guess the slip of paper with contact information was a clue, but this hug told me a lot about how Steel felt about me.

"My real name's Teague. You can call me that."

"Really? Okay." Our private exchange in front of everyone kept growing more awkward.

"She likes her coffee iced." Vander's deep voice vibrated through my body.

Over by the kitchen, he stood holding one of the exact same tumblers from last night, this time filled with ice and brown liquid. I stepped away from Teague and walked over to Vander.

He winked and handed me the cup. I took a huge sip, and everyone in the room stopped talking at once. I felt so self-conscious, if my toes could blush they'd be bright red.

I gulped down my first sip of coffee and struggled to avoid appearing flustered. My gosh, Vander had me all tied up in knots and we hadn't even had breakfast yet.

A few more giant commandos came out of the kitchen carrying snacks and drinks. "Everyone, this is Misha aka Skyler." Vander motioned toward me. They nodded and tipped their chins. What an impressive group of heroes ready for action.

Jade was a lucky girl to work among all these guys. I'd have to ask her about that as soon as I got a chance. I'd bet it was stimulating to say the least.

Vander placed his hand on the small of my back and guided me to a seat next to him on the couch. He leaned forward with his elbows on his knees. "What happened with Kiri?"

"Nothing," Magnum answered. "We followed him to the airport and he left on a flight to Moscow."

Vander nodded. "Good."

"What's the plan," Teague asked.

"She's all in," Vander replied. We hadn't talked about my commitment to leave the Agency explicitly yet, but it appeared he'd received the message.

Teague grinned. "Excellent. Sounds like you guys had a very productive night."

"Zip it, T." Vander sat back and draped his arm behind me on the couch. He seemed so relaxed, a huge difference compared to the robot version of himself. "We need to brainstorm our options to get her out from under their control and safe here with me."

"What elements exactly are we dealing with?" A tall, slim man with sharp defined features spoke to Vander. He had a subtle European accent but I couldn't place it.

"Misha, this is Auggie. He's former Spetsnaz working for Knight Security as our resident Russia expert and all around chameleon."

Auggie dipped his chin at me and waited for me to answer.

I looked down, mortified to admit to this group of honorable men that I had been in bed with criminals my entire adult life. "I am indebted to the SVG under Sergei Medvedev who is associated with the Russian Bratva and the KGB. Ruben Duran and his Colombian drug cartel also have a claim on me. My brother is my handler and is in a similar circumstance."

Vander's teeth clenched, and angry energy bristled from him.

Auggie stared at me unmoving for a moment. I'm sure he was shocked to hear the depth of my entanglement in the dark underworld. People he probably worked daily to bring to justice.

"I'm sorry." I didn't know why I was apologizing. I just felt I had done wrong by these men.

"Misha," Auggie spoke with a soft, deep voice, "No one in this room is without a stain on his record."

I saw a few heads nod and heard one chuckle.

"Particularly me. We're all working day by day to choose the high road, but we've all been where you are. The important part is your commitment to go straight."

"Okay." It seemed impossible but Auggie's words eased my worries. I wasn't broken, just bent, trying to go straight.

Vander's fingertips caressed my upper arm, adding another layer of reassurance. How did I get so lucky to be surrounded by this group? "I am fully committed to leaving if it's possible because I can't fathom returning for another day."

"Good." Auggie looked to Vander. "The first step is to change her identity and give her a new digital footprint."

"Already on it," Vander replied.

Wow. Vander was taking this very seriously.

"Even if I adopt an alias, they'll find me. They'll be relentless because I know so much. Unless they believe I'm dead, they'll never stop."

"So we make you dead," Vander said like it would be easy to kill me, but I'd struggled with this same idea for years.

"It has to be believable."

"We can do that," Teague said.

"How?" I'd helped other SVG agents fake deaths to cover their tracks, but my own I could never pull off.

"They watch her die. The body is never recovered. She's home free." Vander and Teague were on a roll like they'd done this sort of thing many times together.

"I like it." Teague grinned.

"Dangerous as fuck." Axel chimed in.

"I'm down with dangerous as fuck," Jade said with a flash of wickedness in her smile. I liked her and could imagine us being friends.

"It's really not necessary for you all to put yourselves out there like that for me. You barely know me."

"We know you." Magnum spoke directly to me, and I squirmed under his intense gaze. "You're the woman who sacrificed herself for our brother. We got him back, and he's sitting here with us today." He pointed at Teague. "Least we can do is give you a clean start."

Aww. Okay. These guys were all way too kind. I couldn't take it. I didn't deserve it.

"You're one of us now," Axel said to me and I gasped.

"One of you?" Had I heard him correctly?

"The Knight team." Axel nodded.

"Wow." I'd never been part of a team. Always alone, looking out for myself.

Vander beamed.

"Location considerations?" Talon asked the group. Everyone offered ideas, but I couldn't pay attention. One of them? Part of their team? How could this be happening? All because I fell in love with Vander? I assumed many women had fallen in love with him and didn't receive this treatment.

After a long discussion about strategics and risk levels, they'd decided I'd stay here under Vander's protection until the SVG sent a team after me, and we'd make sure they saw me on a boat that exploded while I escaped in the water unseen.

I didn't know how this would work but to a bunch of SEALs, it made perfect sense. They talked about SCUBA gear and submarines.

I took a sip of my iced coffee and thought about last night with Vander. The possessive way he took charge, how I surprised him at his own sneaky ice-in-the-mouth game, and then the rush of warmth that led to the staggering orgasms.

Vander might've sensed me getting turned on because he adjusted his pants and fidgeted in his seat.

I missed a lot of what Vander said because I was thinking about why he'd adjusted his pants, but I thought I'd heard him mention that he'd faked someone's death and pulled it off.

"You've done this before?" I asked him.

"A couple of times."

Wow. I rose up a little, leaned over, and whispered in his ear, "I've done it before too." I gave his lobe a tug with my teeth, not a gentle one, a good hard bite that would leave an impression for hours, then I ran my tongue over it to ease the pinch.

As I pulled away, his eyes widened and slowly slid to mine. His jaw clenched and his hand tightened into a fist, all his muscles going rigid and straining.

Okay. Clearly I'd done something to trip a switch in him. Interesting.

I sat back to find a lot of grinning guys watching. Jade turned her head and smirked. Magnum was full-on laughing and Teague looked... envious? Auggie's eyes lit with mischief as he clasped his hands together tightly. No one spoke. The room filled with awkward silence. Oh boy, I didn't realize everyone was watching us and would react to a small display of affection from me to him. It was just a nip on his ear.

Chapter 33 Mine

Vander cleared his throat. "I need to talk to Misha alone." His voice broke, and he cleared his throat again.

Um, maybe it was a lot more than a nip.

"We'll be right back." He stood and tugged my arm, pulling me back to a home gym/workout room. He slammed the door and sat my butt down on a leather weight bench. It narrowed at the top where there was a bar for sit ups. He placed me at the wider end, spread my legs, and stepped between them. His hand around my neck tilted my head up to look him in the eye. "Do you think if you test me when people are around I won't fuck you right in front of them?"

What? He thought that was a test? "I wasn't testing you. Your ear looked tasty, so I took a bite."

He crouched down and glared into my eyes. His hand slid forward to cup my cheek, his fingers extending into my hair behind my ear and curling in like a scratch. "You can't do that when I'm working. It short circuits my brain."

He was trying to intimidate me, but in the end, he was just a man like all other men. "Aww, poor baby. Can't think with his little captain and his big head at the same time?"

His hands came down and squeezed my thighs like I could listen better if his hands were there. Not. "I am their boss. Their commanding officer. They have never *ever* seen a woman get her mouth anywhere near my ear."

Is that what this was about? How he looked in front of them? "Well they've seen it now, and they all thought it was sexy. Teague and Auggie were jealous as hell. I think it's great if they see this human side of you. Prove you aren't a robot."

His nostrils flared, especially when I mentioned Teague and Auggie. Another switch flipped in his brain. He smashed his lips together and shook his head.

He inhaled a deep breath, and I could see him struggling to get a handle on it. "You are a naughty girl." He grinned and slid his warm hands under my skirt, stopping only when it became too tight. Okay, so he'd gone from mad to flirty in a single breath. This man's moods were driving me batty.

The word *naughty* sparked a long buried need in me. I'd always fantasized about being spanked in a playful way, but never had a man I could trust to do it with. I licked my lips and gazed at him seductively. "Maybe you should spank me."

He stilled, his eyes grew huge and darkened. "Maybe I should."

My stomach flipped. "I would absolutely love it if you spanked me for being naughty." I spread my legs farther and leaned forward, so he could look down my blouse. And look he did. His fingers clenched on my thighs and drifted down toward my core. My legs trembled and a chill raced up my spine.

Were we doing this? We'd done handcuffs and ice cubes and it was phenomenal. He seemed very open to the idea.

He lifted me by the waist and flipped me over so my ass was in the air. "Hold on."

Ooh fun! Yes! We were so doing this. I braced my elbows on the narrow part at the head of the bench. He pulled my hips back and forced my knees together so I was bending at an angle where if I let go, I'd do an epic face plant.

"Have you ever had a good spanking for that mouth?" He caressed my butt over the skirt. From knee up to my back, down again, up again.

I was instantly turned on and wet between my legs. "I've had a lot of bad ones. Never met a man who knew how to do it right." I smiled back at him over my shoulder and gave my butt a little wiggle.

"Oh, sweetheart. I know exactly how to do it." On his way up he lifted my skirt. He had to push hard to get it past my hips, but once he did, my bare behind was exposed. Only a thin black thong protected my private parts. His palm rubbed in a circle on my butt cheek before suddenly drawing down in a slap. It stung a little, but I could tell he was holding back. "Was that the right way?" he asked with a smile.

"I don't know. I'll need to see more first." God, I loved this side of him. So playful and sexy.

He nodded and brought his hand down in another brisk snap. Then another. Right, left, gradually increasing in heft and sting. He stopped to rub the areas with his flat palms and my heated skin tingled where he touched me. "God, I love this ass."

He reached up to pull my undies down and ran a finger through my folds. "You fucking love it."

I couldn't breathe so I didn't answer. I didn't need to. My body answered for me.

He continued, leaving my panties pulled taut around my thighs. This was the most erotic and free I'd ever felt. Each smack drifted closer to my core. I was panting and dying to spread my legs, but the bench was too narrow and my panties wouldn't allow it.

By the time he landed one square on my sensitive lips, I cried out, it felt so good. My back arched and my hips pushed out toward him. "Harder."

As usual, he gave me what I wanted, spanking me harder and giving me more bite in the sting.

"Yes."

He spanked my core several times in quick succession and I held my breath as I absorbed the insane sensation. It felt like all the blood in my body rushed to that one point where his hand connected with the lips of my pussy. I thought I might come from just that.

He yanked my top down and pulled my bra cup. My breasts fell loose for his taking. Oh no. I couldn't handle more stimulation. He pinched my nipple hard and rolled, sending lightning bolts zinging from nipple to clit. His other hand rubbed my right ass cheek in circles and came down in a hard smack that stung and tingled deliciously.

"This ass looks fucking fantastic red from my palm, my naughty girl." His fingers moved to my other nipple and tweaked another lighting bolt down my body. I squirmed as much as I could on the narrow bench with my legs constrained. "No. It's too much. I can't... Oh!"

His mouth came down and his tongue tickled everywhere, leaving a sparkling wet trail in its wake. Up to the crack of my ass, then down between my folds. He curled it up and stabbed it in and out over and over like a man possessed. He arched and licked my clit from behind, teasing it in a wet massage that missed the spot and then hit it dead on. "Oh." So close I could detonate any second now.

His growl sent tantalizing vibrations down to my toes. "You want me to stop?"

"No!" I lowered my cheek to the bench and surrendered to all he was doing. "So good."

His hand reached around my hip and snaked down to my mound. When his fingers brushed my clit, fire burned through my entire body. So hot. "Oh God, yes. More."

"Hush, baby." One hand came up to cover my mouth. His index finger slipped between my lips.

I sucked on his finger and he added another one, tugging my lower lip down and my mouth open.

"You're my goddamn spy. No one else touches you. I can take you wherever I want whenever I want. Even in public, the gym, the kitchen. You won't stop me."

"Uh-huh." I couldn't speak with his fingers in my mouth.

"I can shove my dick in that luscious mouth at my leisure and you'll take it, suck it down like ice cream."

I yanked my lips free of his fingers. "Yes. Now!" I wanted his dick desperately instead of his fingers, but he was withholding it behind me.

"I'll feed it to you later, baby. Don't worry. Bend down and show me what's mine." His hand pressed between my shoulder blades, bringing my ass up higher for him. I heard his pants unbuckle and unzip. I could not wait to feel him on me, in me.

"Yes. That lush ass is so pink and hot for me." He smashed my butt cheeks together and pulled them apart. I loved his rough treatment, every commanding inch of it. I didn't want to be handled like a flower. I was so wet for him. His fingers returned to my clit in a punishing spiral, never slowing, no break, just full-on onslaught, bringing me so high so fast I struggled to keep up.

I felt his hard dick press against the crease of my ass, and his hand slid down so his thumb worked my clit, his fingers plunging deep inside.

One hand reached up and wrapped around my neck to stabilize my shaking body. His thumb strummed my sensitive nub in a flourish like the grand finale in a fireworks show. He brought me higher, higher, to the edge. I couldn't breathe I was so crazed. I moaned obnoxiously loud.

His thumb moved even harder and faster, his hand on my neck supporting my weight, his thick fingertips inside me stimulating nerve bundles I'd never felt before. "Oh!"

My entire body seized, locked in an overwhelming grip of pleasure. I gasped and lurched forward on the bench. He kept me stable as I floated above the room, breathless and blind, riding out my orgasm like a drug. So high. Never ending.

Then his hand was gone from my neck and his giant cock slid between my legs. He entered me in one forceful thrust, stretching my walls until I felt completely filled. His groin smashed into the hot skin of my ass cheeks where he'd spanked me. This wasn't the slow massage of last night's shower or even the teasing with the ice cubes. This was fast dirty fucking with the threat of his team overhearing.

I loved it. Everything about Vander fed into the deep dark fantasies I'd always been afraid to entertain. Sex had become such a chore for me, and with him, it was all about fun and enjoyment. I could finally let go and be myself.

One hand returned to my clit, the other to my neck as he plunged his rock hard cock deep inside. Harder, faster, brutal, all the while extending my orgasm and oh, bringing on another one. "I'm..."

"Yes. Again. Again." His breathless chant behind me tipped me over the edge. Everything contracted around his thrumming cock. He rammed up so deep I felt my chest compress.

When I heard his long groan and felt him spasm, I knew he was coming hard too. We were one body experiencing life's greatest pleasure together. After endless moments locked in suspended bliss, he moved again, drawing out the tail end of it. A few more slower thrusts, and his torso wrapped deeper over my back.

He planted hot kisses on my neck. "Mine." He sunk his teeth into my shoulder and it seemed right. I'd bitten his ear in a sign of possession. Now, he was claiming me.

In my soul, I felt truly his. Someday, the dark cloud over my life would lift, and we'd be together like this whenever we wanted—no fear, no threats. We might both die fighting to make it happen, but what would our lives be like if we didn't try? I knew mine wouldn't be worth living, so if Vander and his team wanted to risk it for me, I'd help them and do my best to make the mission successful.

He nipped my ear and spoke with a hoarse voice. "Promise me one thing."

"Anything." I turned my head and he pulled a long sensual kiss from my lips.

"Never sacrifice yourself for me again."

I gasped and closed my eyes. That was a lot to ask and I was lost in post-orgasmic haze. We were still joined down below.

"Van..."

"I don't need you to die for me, I need you to live for me."

What could I say to that? He needed this promise from me, and I could not deny him anything.

"Okay."

"Say it."

"I won't sacrifice myself for you."

"Good." He kissed me again and I wanted to ask him to promise the same, but he pulled out and I gasped at the loss. "We have to clean up and get back to the meeting." He slipped my panties back up for me.

"Do you think they heard?" I peeled my sweaty arms and knees off the bench.

"Don't care." He walked me over to the bathroom and we cleaned up, both of us grinning. Time to face my team.

Chapter 34 Black

Vander

After six weeks in lockdown with Misha, I'd completely surrendered my heart to her. We spent the first two weeks fucking with a little bit of talking between orgasms.

We finally climbed out of bed and attempted to construct some sort of "normal" routine. Three meals a day, working out, various forms of entertainment that didn't involve my cock and her pussy. Although that was still my favorite form of entertainment and would probably always be. I worked from home and delegated a lot of my load at the office. We held twice daily meetings with the team to discuss any new intel on Sergei, Kiri, and Duran.

We made plans to travel together after this was all over. She wanted Blue to learn to pull a sled, wanted to see me in action in the snow. We talked endlessly about my family, what I could tell her of my past that wasn't classified, the escort business, which she hadn't given up her morbid curiosity about, and the kind of life she wanted after we'd freed her.

Now it was oh-dark-thirty and Blue whimpered for his walk. We'd neglected to take him out after dinner, hoping he'd use his patch of grass on the balcony, but he'd refused and now we were paying for it.

"I'm gonna take Blue out." I kissed her shoulder and got up to pull on some clothes.

"I'll go with you." She was face down naked in the bed, about to drift off to sleep.

"Nope. Stay."

We'd been overly cautious with her, keeping her inside, but it was beginning to look like they weren't going to come for her and we'd have to go to them. I didn't like putting her out there like that, but it might be necessary and she could certainly handle it.

"One more week. If they don't approach, we implement Plan B."

She grunted a quiet assent. We'd talked through the details of a plan to move the mission to Moscow. It was a lot more complicated, but could still be executed cleanly. "The good news is your brother has proven trustworthy so far. There's no evidence he's revealed your location."

"Kiri's a good person. He's caught up in the same web as I am. He lost his parents too."

At the door, I checked and holstered my S&W .45, grabbed my knife, a flashlight, and the leash.

Blue bounded over and I hooked the leash to his collar.

I called Magnum up on the comms and popped the microphone bud into my ear as we entered the elevator.

"Sup." Magnum sounded sleepy.

"Wake your ass up. I'm going out to walk the dog."

"I gotta wake my ass up because Blue has to take a shit?"

"No. You wake your ass up because I'll fuck you up if you don't cover me right now." The elevator opened and I walked Blue through the empty lobby. When we hit the street, Magnum said, "Gotcha. Spotted you from my balcony. It's cold as hell. Get your business done and get back up."

"Get yourself a jacket, you wimp." It was not cold as hell. Unless you'd spent a winter in Alaska, you didn't know what cold as hell felt like. Fifty degrees and clear skies was a balmy day in Alaska.

Blue pulled because he wanted to run off the leash and chase some night crawlers he heard in the bushes. "We all want to run free, Blue. Not yet."

"Spotted a laser on the dog?" Magnum's urgent voice turned up in question.

Blue was six feet out. An orange dot on Blue's flank. Shit.

I dove for the dog. He yelped as I landed on top of him and rolled him toward the side of the building. An orange dot meant sniper which would be harder to spot in the dark and my .45 was useless.

"Mag. You got a sight on him?"

"No. The team's activated. Be there in sixty."

Sixty seconds was a long time for a sniper to aim and fire at an open target pinned to a wall. I got one foot under me and tucked Blue to my chest. I was moving him deeper into cover.

An orange dot on my hip. A trace. Sharp pain. Shit. I went down. My leg. Shit. Fuck. "I'm hit." Blue was under me so he was safe. "Get to Misha quick. Secure her in the safe room."

"Vander!" Misha bolted out of the building with her rifle up. Fuck! No! What the hell was she doing? She ran along the wall toward me, searching the windows above for the sniper.

"No! Go back!"

Cars approached, footsteps, yelling, rapid fire, her blurry form hitting the sidewalk. More shots down the street, from the lobby. Over my head. My team was in an active firefight, and I didn't have the strength or control to raise my weapon.

I lay helpless on the pavement, bleeding out as they dragged her limp body into a vehicle. Axel, Magnum, several others around the corner fired at the car. My mouth wouldn't open. Like a nightmare where you're underwater and can't breathe. *Follow them. Don't lose sight of her.* My muscles failed. Nothing. I could do nothing. My world went black.

***

Holed up in bed for a damn week. Seven days I could've been out looking for her. Precious time lost. At least the teams were on it full force. All my available operators were either in San Diego, Moscow, or Cartagena following leads. Keegan had assembled a team of expert hackers and had plenty of backup ready to go once we got the call to move, if it ever came.

The grief and worry from my brother's capture shadowed over every moment of my recovery. The only reason we'd found him was because of her. Now, she was in danger and we didn't have a contact like her to help us. Except Kiri. Kiri was the missing link in all of this. If we could make contact, we could convince him to save his sister if she was still alive.

If she was dead, the team would have to hold me back from an international murder spree. She was too good to die and so close to her first chance at freedom. I could not lose the only woman I'd ever loved.

London checked the bandage on my leg again. "You have to relax. The stress is preventing your wound from healing. I can give you something to help you sleep."

"No. I'm fine. If something goes down, I don't wanna be drugged up."

"If something goes down, you'd be useless in this condition. You need to heal for her."

"Don't need any reminders that I'm useless right now, London." I didn't even have the energy to get angry at him.

"Sorry. My point is that you'll recover faster if you can find a way to manage the stress."

When I closed my eyes, the visions taunted me. Her as a prisoner, tortured with hot water, her regrets about the decisions she made to be with me, the way she must feel so disappointed in me for allowing her to be captured after I'd promised to protect her.

I kept seeing her brother's face laughing with no remorse. My gut told me he harbored vindictive jealousy against her and he would use the situation to bring her down, but she'd insisted he was on her side.

I hated being dependent on an unknown. To help calm the chaos inside, I imagined her voice talking about her drawings, her laugh when I tickled her, her smile everytime she reunited with Blue.

The phone I'd been using to contact Kiri finally buzzed.

"Knight."

"Vander? It's Kiri." The worry in his voice could be good for us. We wanted him on our side.

"Where is she?"

"She's in Cartagena. Duran's had her for a week." Duran had her. Not what I expected, but slightly better because Duran was a known entity. We had very little intel on Sergei and the SVG. "How soon can you get here?" Kiri asked me.

"I have men on the ground there."

"Good. We have to hurry." Kiri sounded desperate for my help. I couldn't tell if it was genuine or not. Did he truly care about his sister or was he eager to lure me into a trap?

"What's the situation?"

"Duran has Misha. Sergei wants me to rescue her and then kill her. I can do the rescue part, but I told them I didn't want to kill her."

"Why do they want to kill her?"

"She's lost all trust with them. She shouldn't have gone to see you. I had it all worked out."

"Yeah, but your solution didn't work for her."

"Send your man to Avendia San Martin. Plaza Pierino Gallo. Let me know when he's here."

I did not like Kiri giving me orders at all.

"It's sketchy, Kiri. How do I know it's not a trap?"

"I don't even know if Sergei is sending me into a trap. I'm taking a chance calling you. Get here ASAP. Bring guns and explosives and we'll blast her out." Again with the handing out orders like he knew anything about me.

"I'll be there in less than twenty-four hours. Keep her safe until I'm there. I mean it. This is your one job. Keep her safe."

"Duran has her. I think she's safe with him for now. I can't protect her from the outside. There are guards." He let out a long sigh like this had been weighing on him.

"Okay. Then don't do anything. Stay put until we've made contact."

"Hurry. I can only stall Sergei for so long." Once again, he sounded fishy.

"If you're gaming me, you're dead."

"No. I wouldn't risk her life that way. I need your help and fast." For the first time, I got the feeling we could trust Kiri based on the honesty of his response. Of course, he was an expert liar, so there was no way to know for sure except go there and test him.

"On our way."

I ended the call and looked at London. "Let's mobilize."

"Your injury."

"I'm fine." Suddenly it didn't hurt anymore, and hopeful energy fueled me. We could do this. We'd done it before. "I have an idea that should work. It all depends on Kiri. I'm betting on him to come through for her."

"That's a rough bet."

"All we got. Let's mobilize."

Chapter 35 Heart's Desire

Misha

I'd been mostly left alone for the last week. Duran's men kept me in a small room and brought me food. I had a toilet, a sheet, and a blanket. The window was cased in concrete and couldn't be breached. They didn't beat me, torture me, question me, or talk to me.

The entire week was spent calling on my training to avoid going insane. Whenever the fear and anxiety swelled up, I turned my focus inward. Vander. Blue. The rocking of a yacht on the water, the rocking of his hips, the rough yet controlled touch of his kiss, his deep rich voice.

I promise to protect you.

No matter what, I didn't allow my thoughts to wander to his massive body lying on the ground, blood seeping from his leg. No thoughts of his death or his lifeless body were allowed to plant seeds because that would weaken me beyond repair, and I could not give in to the fatalistic thoughts that plagued me.

Today, Duran had decided to change the situation. Perhaps he needed to prove his machismo with me or maybe he needed a week to make sure it was safe to meet with me. Maybe he was so busy he couldn't make time in his schedule to release me from my detention.

The guards delivered me to one of his villas in the hills. They were noticeably not rough with me. Duran's mouth turned down as they tied me to a chair, hands behind my back. He looked weary and stressed out. His face pale and his hair long. He held a small pistol in his hand, but he wasn't pointing it at me.

"Why were you with the Navy SEAL and his brother?" he asked me in Spanish.

Ahh, yes. He was worried about Vander and his team as he should be. They would destroy him if they got close enough. Shoot. They could probably sniper him out through his living room window from two hundred yards.

When I didn't answer, he slapped my face. Not hard. More of a warning strike.

"Are they coming after me for the hostage thing?"

He was living in fear of retaliation for the trick he'd played on Vander. It was a stupid move and it would cost him his life. He knew he was at risk, and was desperately trying to get me to solve this for him.

I clenched my teeth and prepared for another blow when I didn't answer, but it didn't come. Maybe Ruben was going easy on me because I was a woman, maybe he had one shred of decency in him or he felt a tiny bit of guilt about the burns on my back.

I focused on the wall as Ruben walked around me. I imagined an explosive breaching that wall, a team of men marching in to save me.

But Vander wouldn't come for me this time. If he was dead, I would beg Ruben to kill me. Teague and his team would be devastated. Vander was their fearless leader, their brother, the point of the spear. If he died to protect me, I deserved to die. The guilt would be the end of me. If Ruben didn't kill me, I could easily get Sergei to do it.

Vander's voice came to me again.

I need you to live for me, not die for me.

You know what I do when someone tells me I can't do something? I work like hell to prove them wrong.

His dark rasp sounded clear like he was standing in the room. Hearing his voice triggered something in me. Maybe I could be with Vander again if I mustered some grit as Teague had said.

It seemed impossible now, but I believed in Vander and Teague with all my heart. If Vander was alive, he'd be looking for me. If he'd died, Teague and the team would still be looking for me. Even Kiri could come through. Ruben might not kill me, and I could evade and escape.

It was a tiny sliver of hope, but I clung to it like a balloon, lifting me out of my despair to a point where I could think straight. I had to keep fighting to stay alive for him in case he came for me.

I needed to play every card in my hand with Ruben. Hopefully, he still loved me. My old faithful defense with men like him. I couldn't defeat him if he held a gun to my head, but I had a chance if I could get him to feel compassion for me.

"Please, Ruben. Do you remember how we made love? It was good. I wasn't faking it." I was totally faking it, and I hated every second his putrid flesh touched my skin, but I would say anything to make him vulnerable so I could escape.

He stopped walking and stared at me with a pinched eyebrow. He didn't know what to make of me. Good. "Did you ever truly love me?" he asked.

Yes! This was a good turn. "I did." I did not, but I loved that he was begging me to reassure him. It shifted the power back over to my side.

He stepped in front of me and glared down. "I wanted to believe your brother that you had confessed your crimes because the Americans forced you to do it."

Anything he wanted to believe, I would do everything I could to convince him it was true. "Yes. He didn't lie. I didn't really tell them anything. They told me to tell you I had. They threatened my brother if I didn't do it. It's true. This is all just a misunderstanding. Please release me." I raised my bound hands and looked over my shoulder with pain on my face, showing him how uncomfortable I was. He should be eager to please me if he wanted me to love him.

"We didn't expect to find you with the American special ops team in San Diego. We simply wanted to talk to them to clear things up."

"I believe you." Yeah, right. Colombian drug lords didn't have talks to clear things up. They had gun fights and drive-by assassinations. However, if they hadn't expected to see me, I may have saved Vander's life by providing a distraction.

He kneeled down and squeezed my knees. "Why were you there? Please tell me so I can let you go."

"Same reasons as you. I felt we had unfinished business and we had to clear things up. I told them I was furious they forced me to sacrifice myself. I wanted him to apologize because I was tortured for that. Your man Angel poured boiling water on my back and scarred my skin."

He flinched back and his eyes filled with sympathy. "I wasn't aware of that, my love. I would never have allowed it. Did he apologize to you? Because I do. I'm so sorry he hurt you."

Yes. I had this man wrapped around my finger. I was too darn good at this. "Please untie me. I'll show you the burns and you can make it better."

"I can't erase what's passed." He looked down and shook his head.

"No, but if you apologize, it will heal me. I want to feel your embrace again, Ruben. You must untie me now that we have confessed to each other and shared our true heart's desire. I want to be with you forever if you'll have me." I plastered on an empathetic smile for him. I put on my mask, stifled my soul, and truly looked at this man like I wanted him as I had been taught since I was a child. If your eyes are honest and you appeal to his deepest needs, a man will give you anything.

"I could only keep you as a mistress. My wife is my female companion in public."

Gross. "I understand. Anything so I could be with you. Please release me. I want to kiss you." I parted my lips and leaned toward him.

He grinned, happy with himself, and cut through the rope around my wrists. The blood rushed to my fingertips as I shook out my hands.

"Thank you." I sighed and smiled.

His eyes darkened. He was ready to collect. He expected me to sleep with him. He didn't expect me to swipe his gun when he leaned in for a kiss. I got a hold of it and aimed it at his head.

His face fell. "Mi amor, you betray me?" He sounded genuinely disappointed he wasn't going to get laid.

"Sit in the chair."

"We can talk this through."

"Sit in the chair or you die."

Chapter 36 Witnesses

As he walked to the chair, a clattering boom echoed through the walls. Something was going on downstairs. Loud shots rang out, both muted and unmuted. Ruben's men against Vander's? Vander's team would use silencers.

My heart pounded so hard in my chest I could barely hear what was happening. Footsteps ran up the stairs and burst through the door. I aimed my weapon at the intruder. Ruben turned to see who had come in and came face-to-face with a masked man and his rifle. Just like that first night in Colombia, and many times since then, Vander was standing in front of me prepared to defend me.

My heart flew through the roof. He wasn't dead. He came for me like he'd said he would.

Vander's gaze moved from Ruben to me. He took in my exhausted body, my red face, the dirt on my clothes. He turned back to Ruben and didn't hesitate.

He fired and shot Ruben straight through the heart. He fell instantly. It all happened in less than a heartbeat, but it felt like slow-motion.

Vander had come in and shot an unarmed man without a second thought. By the severe look in his eyes, he wasn't going to give it a second thought anytime soon. "Can you run?" he asked me.

"Yes." I remembered the pain of how he carried me last time. Luckily this time, I was better off and I had my own weapon. Well, I had Ruben's weapon.

"Let's move." He made sure I was close behind him as he took the lead out of the room and down the stairs. Urgent but not hurried. Confidence under fire. Very sexy.

After a week in prison with very little sleep, I felt like I was running through a black hole, but I followed his back and did my best to stay alert.

I stumbled on the last step, but he covered me, scanning the room for threats.

His teammates, also masked, came down one of the hallways and met us. "Clear."

"Move."

I followed Vander and they fell in line behind us. I was part of the team again.

We emerged into the night air and ran to a van parked outside.

We all filed into the back of the van and took off down the street. I couldn't see who was driving but I thought it might be Axel.

This was all too easy, and I couldn't help feeling like more challenges awaited us.

Vander wrapped his arm around my neck. "Down, Kroshka."

I sighed and fell to my hands and knees. "It feels so good to hear your voice again."

"Same for you, sweetheart. Same." He leaned in to kiss my cheek and I tilted my head. Our lips brushed but the van wobbled and tossed us around.

"We're taking fire," Axel called from the driver's seat.

Someone in the passenger seat rolled down his window and returned fire.

"How many?" Vander asked.

"At least five," a female voice replied. Jade.

"That's good. More witnesses," Vander said inexplicably.

"What's going on?" I asked.

A loud pop rang out and the van tilted to the side. Vander's body slid on top of mine as we spun out. He groaned.

"Are you in pain?" I asked him.

More shots pinged the walls of the van.

"Keep going. We need to make it to the harbor."

"Tire blew out." Axel stated the obvious.

"Drive on the rims! Don't stop until we're at the harbor."

The van revved and accelerated. We slid against the back door as the van hobbled along the street. The metal of the wheels screeched as it rubbed the road.

More rounds popped through the metal walls until they were like Swiss cheese.

After another minute of the slowest car chase ever, we stopped and hopped out while the team in the van covered us. We ran to a dock with a man standing at the entrance.

"Kiri?" My brother was standing there. What was his part in this?

He brought up a rifle and aimed it at me.

"Kiri, no!"

Vander stood in front of me and aimed his rifle at him.

"I'm sorry, Misha. I have to do this," my brother said.

"You don't. Come with us." Our pursuers were closing in, but I assumed we would escape on the yacht at the end of the dock.

"I can't go with you but I want you to have a happy life. Promise me you'll be happy." His face was drawn and tortured as he tilted his head slightly for us to run.

"I promise." I held back tears and ran down the dock with Vander behind me. My brother fired at us but missed. He must've missed on purpose because he was a good shot.

Vander's team was holding off the attackers back at the van. I saw at least three of the men who were chasing us fall dead on the street. We made it onto the boat, both of us struggling to breathe. Vander loosened the mooring ropes and cast off from the pier. I glanced back at my brother one last time before we disappeared below deck.

We raced down a narrow corridor and stopped at the docking pad to a small submarine.

"Get in quick."

I climbed in and Vander grimaced as he followed behind me. Steel said hello with a smile, and Magnum waved from the cockpit. The eerie quiet of the submarine shocked my system compared to the chaos we'd just left behind.

We strapped on seat belts and Vander leaned his head back. "Ready for launch."

"We're doing this?" I asked him.

"Hopefully soon before your brother blows us up." He closed his eyes.

"My brother?"

"He has the detonator."

"Why?"

"It has to look like he did it."

Look like. "You're not... We're not..."

"Hopefully, you'll be dead in the next few minutes."

"You're kidding me."

"Not a joking man, Kroshka. Not about stuff like this."

"Okay."

The submarine's engine vibrated below us, and my stomach sank as we descended. Through the porthole, sea water rose and engulfed us. An enormous blast thundered behind us and vibrated through the submarine. The water deadened the noise but didn't stop the vessel from pitching forward before it corrected.

"Boom." Vander's hands fanned out in a circle. "You're dead." He smiled like a drunken fool before he closed his eyes again.

"Was that Honor?" I asked Magnum.

"No. That's another yacht." He waved a hand like it was no big deal that they had just blown up a yacht in a harbor in Categena, Colombia.

"You blew up someone else's yacht?"

Magnum chuckled. "Yeah."

Did nothing phase that man?

"Technically, Kiri did it," Teague added.

"Will he be okay?"

Vander grabbed my hand and peeked out the porthole. "If we pulled it off, the SVC thinks he killed you and he should be safe. If not, he deals with it. Not you."

I peered out the porthole, as if I could see Kiri up on the dock from under the surface of the water. "That's who was following us?"

"Yes. Kiri set it all up." Vander wrapped a strong arm around my neck and pulled my face closer. "He gave you this. He wants you to be free. It's your turn. Take it."

"What about your team?" We'd left them up on the dock to face down the SVC.

"They'll be all right."

"I can't believe we got away with it."

"I can't believe Kiri came through for you."

"No sign of anyone tailing us," Axel said from the cockpit.

"This is so awesome. I think they'll fall for it. I believed the whole thing. It looked so real!" I jumped on him and wrapped my arms around his neck. He grunted and steadied me with his hand. "Oh, sorry. You're injured."

"I'm healed now, baby. Totally healed." He leaned back and hissed through the pain. His arm snaked tighter around my neck and pulled me in for a soft kiss. We embraced in an awkward hug in the tiny seats of the submarine as we flew through the water like a small whale.

"Thank you, Vander. Thank you for doing all of this for me." I peppered his face with kisses. Magnum and Steel laughed in the front of the submarine.

"The least I can do after all you've done for me." His voice sounded pained. We needed to get him some medical care, but I had a feeling he'd be all right.

"We saved each other," I said.

"Absolutely, we did."

Chapter 37 Atlanta

We flew to Atlanta on a chartered jet and quietly made our way through the airport before the sun came up, trying not to attract any attention. Although, walking around with a group of huge men and one badass woman at four in the morning did turn some heads. They'd all changed into street clothes, but still looked like the cast of Star Wars walking out of the Millenium Falcon after a battle.

Vander's brother Keegan aka Maverick set us up in a safe house outside the city. It looked like an ordinary apartment, but Keegan and Vander said it was secure. No one would find us here. Vander slept most of the flight over, and London put him on bed rest and painkillers as soon as we were settled in the safe house.

I stayed by his side, bringing him water and food, wiping his brow, holding his hand. He would wake up and smile at me, say I love you, then pass out again. He wouldn't let me help him walk to the bathroom, but he managed that on his own. Blue kept vigil next to him on the bed.

In the middle of the afternoon, he sat up and frantically patted at the bed, twisting and turning at the waist to look for something. Blue hopped off the bed and executed a massive shake after being disturbed. "My gun."

"Shh, Van. It's all right. You don't need your gun. We're safe here. We're in Atlanta. I'm here. Teague is here. We're all safe. It's over."

Even though he wasn't fully awake, he nodded, placed a hand on my thigh and went back to sleep.

Later that night, Vander woke again. This time calmer. More alert. "Hey, babe," he said to me out of the corner of his mouth as it turned up in a small grin.

"Hey. You feeling better?"

"Yeah." He reached for my hand and pulled me in for a kiss. "Thank you for staying by my side."

"London says you're going to be okay. Just needed the rest."

He nodded and his arm snaked out behind my back. He motioned for me to climb in next to him. I did, careful not to hurt him, and rested my head on his shoulder near his armpit. My other hand pressed over his heart.

He wasn't having that distance between us and scooped me up until my side was plastered to his and my leg draped over his knees. "That's better."

"Does it still hurt?"

"Not anymore." He smiled and my heart did a little pitter patter.

We stayed like that for a long while. When he didn't fall back to sleep, I assumed it was okay to start a conversation. "I'm sorry I left the building that night," I said.

"No."

I arched my neck to look up at him. "No?"

"Lets not do that. First off, you're not really sorry because you would do it again."

I returned my head to our cuddling position. "I would."

"It was wrong of me to ask you to make a promise you couldn't keep. It's who you are and that's the woman I love." He stroked my hair out of my face and smoothed it down my back. His touch left a warm trace down my spine. I needed to ask London when Vander would be cleared for sexual activities. Or maybe it didn't matter because Vander wouldn't follow doctor's orders anyway.

"In the same light, I assume I won't be able to ask you to promise me you won't risk your life for mine?" I asked him.

"Nope. We are who we are. Shaken and stirred with a hint of danger." His hand traveled lower and his fingertips grazed over the curve of my butt.

"It's been a lot more than a hint lately."

"The worst is behind us. Don't know what's ahead." He pushed with his hands to sit up in the bed and grimaced with the pain.

"No, stay."

"I've been down long enough. I always get back up." He situated the pillow behind his back then his arm came around and he swung me over, forcing me to straddle him. "You want to keep working?"

"Do I have a choice?"

"Babe." He leveled his sleepy sexy gaze on me. "You don't need to work. You can take up a hobby, lay by the pool all day, anything you want."

Hmm. That sounded nice. "Draw?"

"Absolutely anything."

I chewed my lip and pondered what he'd said. His gaze moved to my lips and watched the movement. "I'm not really a lay by the pool kind of girl."

"Nope. Another reason I love you."

"Okay, so I need to find a job." I tapped my fingers on his chest. I didn't really have any skills that would work in retail or even in an office. "Law enforcement?"

He shrugged. "If that's what you want."

"I'll never pass the security clearance."

"If you want to be a cop, I know enough people I could get you into the academy." He ran his hands up and down my thighs, distracting me while we were having a very important conversation.

At the word "academy" I flinched and stopped his hands. "I don't think I could ever go to another academy."

"Right. Auggie mentioned the CIA might be interested in your skills if you wanted to be a double agent."

A sour taste filled my mouth. "Nothing with the word *agent* in it either."

He nodded. "What do you truly desire?"

"I desire your humongous cock." I slid my hips forward and teased him. He wasn't fully hard yet, but getting there.

"You got that already, but I do need to take my ass, and my cock, to work sometimes. Got over 1,000 employees."

I gasped. "Knight Security is that big?"

"That's just my division. West Coast. My brothers run a similar operation on the East Coast."

"Wow. I'm impressed. Okay then. I know what I truly desire."

"Uh oh." He chuckled.

"I want to work for Knight Security. I have the skills. We could work together. It would be challenging and exciting. I would love more than anything to officially be part of the team."

His hand came up to cup my cheek, and his eyes went through a whole series of emotions. I couldn't tell what they were, but my choice had stirred something warm in him. "It would be my honor to have a woman of your caliber working with me."

My heart melted down to my toes. A woman of my caliber? No one had ever... "With you? Not for you?"

"Babe. You're my queen. I can't employ you. We'd have to work it out with my brothers, but you'd come in at the top."

"I don't need that."

"I know what you need and I'm giving it to you, remember?"

"What I need more than anything is to earn my rank, not by sleeping with someone, so I'd like to come in at entry level. No special treatment because I'm screwing the boss."

His eyes assessed me then softened. "You can start at Knight Security at any level if that's what you want."

I pressed my lips together and stifled a sob. "More than anything."

"Then it's done." His hands caressed my butt and lifted me up onto his cock, which was more than fully hard now. "We'll negotiate the details later." He kissed me and started rocking me against him.

Warm tingles spread through my entire being. "We should keep it to just this." I looked down at where we were pressed together.

His lips quirked. "Just this?" He rocked me harder against his dick and my stomach flip-flopped. My nipples pebbled. I felt wet between my legs. I was losing this battle already.

"Yes," was my breathy reply.

"We all know how that worked out." He skimmed a hand up my side and his thumb teased the underside of my breast.

"It worked out really good for me." I laughed.

"Me too."

And then we did a lot more than *just this* and many things I'm sure were against doctor's orders, but we didn't care. We were in love, and we couldn't hold back any longer.

Epilogue Snow Dog

Six months later

Vander

Snow sprayed out behind us as we mushed through the Great North Woods of New Hampshire.

I'd hired a sled dog team to guide us on a three day expedition. Ten gorgeous huskies pulled us in a sled where my Misha, who was now my Celeste, sat in the carriage and I stood behind, calling to the dogs.

Blue was tied to the side near me for much of the trip, but since he wasn't conditioned for long races, he often sat in the sled with Misha and enjoyed the ride. He barked orders at the other dogs like he was the musher.

They barked back like they were telling the cocky puppy to shut the hell up. Blue had a long way to go before he could even think of joining a professional team like this.

The expedition company followed a mile behind us as guides and when we stopped, they took care of the dogs, but mostly they let us be so we could experience being alone in the wilderness together.

This was my idea of a vacation. When Misha said she wanted to see Blue pull a sled, she didn't know we'd end up on a sixty-mile trek through New England. But she needed to know that when she signed up with me, she got to experience life large and unleashed.

We were on day two and deep into the forest. She didn't know it, but I had a surprise planned for her.

Out in the middle of nowhere, when we hit the turn, I tipped the sled on purpose.

The dogs stopped running, and the sled came to a halt in the snow.

Misha got out to help me right the sled, but I stopped her. "What was that?"

"What?"

"I heard something. Like a growl." I grabbed my shotgun from the sled and stomped away from the trail.

"Vander. Do not go hunting down a bear right now."

"He could hurt you or the dogs. We have to go get him."

"No, no, we don't. We do not need to go get that bear right now." The nervous quiver in her voice made me laugh.

"You stay here." I knew she wouldn't, so I threw that in there.

She grabbed Blue's lead and followed me into the deep snow drift, her legs struggling each time she sank in deep, her boots covered in snow. Blue was excited to go exploring. "Vander, please come back. Is this some kind of Legends of the Fall thing where you need to challenge the bear who scarred your face?"

I chuckled. "No. That bear's dead. I don't hold a grudge."

Through the trees, my surprise for her came into view.

A large-scale igloo complete with entry portico and all the accommodations. It looked fantastic in the small clearing.

"Oh my God." She stopped dead in her tracks. Her face was priceless. Mouth open, leaning forward in shock. "What the heck is this?"

"It's a castle for my queen."

"For us?"

"Well, yeah. Go check it out."

She bent down and crouched through the arched entry. Inside, I'd set up a warming plate, a sleeping bag on a raised cot, big enough for us to share but small enough to keep her on top of me, a meal we just had to heat and eat, and a string of lights up on the wall. "I cannot believe this. It's spectacular."

The ice walls cast a light-blue tint to the space. "It is pretty cool." Blue sniffed around the edges and then got stuck on the food. I shooed him off of it.

"Did you make this by yourself? When?"

"No. The expedition team helped. I had my team up here too working on it."

"You had a team of Navy SEALs build us a romantic igloo?"

"Sure. Good practice for them for snow conditions. If they ever get stranded, they'll know how to build themselves a pimped-out shelter. Maybe they'll get lucky and find themselves a baby seal to cuddle with." I wiggled my eyebrows.

With that, she doubled over laughing. It was a beautiful sound anytime Misha laughed, and she'd been doing it a lot more lately. We were close to certain now that the SVG had signed off on her death, and Duran's men were not seeking retaliation. Kiri even provided body parts with matching DNA and dental records. Sergei held a funeral for her and never mentioned any doubt to Kiri. He played the role of the grieving brother and received accolades for his valor and loyalty.

"Sit down and relax."

She grinned as she carefully took a seat on the cot that supported the bed.

"Champagne?"

"Vander. What is going on here?"

"When we're old and gray, we'll tell our grandkids about this igloo."

"Grandkids?"

I bent low and walked over to her. I took her hand and dropped to one knee in the snow. "We'll tell them all about the day I asked you to marry me."

She sucked in a huge, loud breath and covered her eyes with her hands. "No, no, no, no."

"Was hoping to hear a yes, babe." I tilted my head to see behind her hands. "C'mon. Talk to me."

She lowered her hands and she had tears in her eyes, her face red, her upper lip quivering. My rock of a woman was about to cry. We hadn't talked about marriage at all. I wanted to surprise her. Looked like I'd accomplished that. I laughed at her total loss of composure. She'd better say yes soon, or I'd be losing mine too.

"Blue. Come here."

Blue sauntered over, tongue hanging out, excited and panting.

"He has your ring."

"He does? Where?"

"He's been wearing it this whole time on his collar. Open the pocket."

Her hands shook as she reached for him and fumbled with the pocket. I wanted her to be the one to remove it from his collar, but she was not in any shape to perform fine motor skills.

"You can face down a SEAL team with your rifle, but you fall apart when I ask you to marry me?" I fished the ring out of the pocket on Blue's collar. He looked very happy to be a part of whatever was going on.

"Yes. Gosh, Vander. Don't tease me. I'm trying to absorb it. You sprung all this on me with no warning."

"Such will be your life if you say yes."

She nodded and tears fell down her face.

"I need to hear you say it, loud and clear." I held up the ring and it gleamed in the light-blue glow of the igloo. A beautiful four-carat princess-cut diamond that Jade helped me pick out. Her wide eyes were glued to it. "Will you pledge your love to me and me alone for all your living days until death and beyond?"

"Yes," she breathed.

"Say the whole thing. Louder. Yes, Vander. I pledge..."

She threw her head back and took a deep breath. She looked me in the eye and said what I'd been waiting to hear. "Yes, Vander. I pledge my love to you and you alone for all my living days until death and beyond."

"That's all I need to know." I took her mouth with mine and sealed the deal. Cold on the outside, hot on the inside. My queen would be mine forever. It felt incredibly good to know this.

"Do you pledge too?" she asked me after a long time kissing right before I was about to take her on the cot and rip off all her layers of protection to get to my girl's luscious body under there.

I paused and looked into her eyes. "I pledge that I am yours. Body and soul. Head to toe. Future and past. I've never loved anyone like I love you and never will love anyone else. You're my soulmate. My one true love." Her face crumbled as I spoke.

"Now can we get to the fucking because I'm much better at that than all this romantic shit."

She grinned. "Yes."

It took me ten minutes to get us both naked, but once we were, we celebrated in our own special way. It was official. Misha was mine forever.

###

Playlist

"Baby Come Back" by Player

    "Black" by Dierks Bentley

    "Despacito" by Luis Fonsi ft. Daddy Yankee

    "Fall In Line" by Christina Aguilera feat. Demi Lovato

    "Forever After All" by Luke Combs

    "Hold My Hand" Hootie and the Blowfish

    "If You Were Mine" by Ocean Park Standoff ft. Lil Yachty

    "Just Give Me a Reason" by P!nk ft. Nate Ruess

    "Little One" by Highly Suspect

    "You & Me" by Peder B. Helland

Other Books by Bex Dane

Men of Siege Series

    Violet (0.5) Get it free at bexdane.com

    Rogan (1)

    Tessa (1.4) Get it free at bexdane.com

    Lachlan (1.5)

    Zook (2)

    Torrez (3)

    Falcon (4)

    Men of Siege Box Set (Books 1-4)

    Twist Brothers Series

    Fighting for Foster (0.5)

    Captivated by Cutter (1)

    Memorizing Mace (2)

    Twist Brother Box Set (Books 0.5 - 2)

    Knight Security Series

    Blue Honor (This book)

    Steel Valor (2)

    Safe Harbor (3)

    Knight Security Box Set (Books 1-3)

Visit bexdane.com to sign up to Bex Dane's mailing list. You'll receive free books, bonus content, and updates on all Bex's new releases.

Printed in Great Britain
by Amazon